# RETURN TO ME

## THE PRIDE SERIES

## JILL SANDERS

GRAYTON

*To my family,*
*who have always been there for me.*

# SUMMARY

Becca and Nick were destined to be together. He was the love of her life, or so she thought. Then tragedy strikes, and Becca is left heartbroken and devastated. The road to recovery seems almost hopeless at times, but with love and support from the good people of Pride, she's looking forward to putting the past behind her. When Nick's best friend, Sean, returns home a year later, he brings with him an unexpected gift and she relives the past all over again.

Sean's homecoming is tarnished by the loss of his best friend and the recent discovery of his fiancée's infidelities while he was deployed. If Sean needs anything right now, it's a good friend to lean on, and Becca has always been there for him. When the two decide to get away for a while, they're forced to accept the undeniable attraction between them. But now an unforeseen challenge threatens to rip them apart forever.

# PROLOGUE

*B*ecca waited under the big oak tree for what seemed like hours. It was the eve of her sixteenth birthday, and Nick had promised that he'd give her a birthday gift early. She'd snuck out tonight, much like she'd been doing on and off for the past year.

Her mother seemed too busy to even notice or care what she was doing lately. Half the time, Becca had to fend for herself for meals, hunting something to eat at home or running down to a friend's house and bumming a meal off them.

At least her mother had stopped smoking in the last few years. It was wonderful not to have to hide the smell of smoke on her clothes anymore. She'd become accustomed to dousing herself with perfume just before walking out the door, and now she didn't have to.

Her sister, Sara, had left for Portland a while back. She hated to admit it, but she really missed having her around. Sara had always been a wonderful cook. Becca really missed a good meal.

Sighing, she looked down at her phone and frowned. Nick was supposed to be here at eleven thirty, but it was almost a quarter to midnight. Just then, she heard a branch snap not far away.

"Nick?" she whispered. "Is that you?"

"Who else would be coming to see you?" He chuckled as he walked forward. "Sorry I'm late. My dad was up watching the news, and I had to wait until he went to bed."

She wrapped her arms around his shoulders and kissed him. "You're forgiven, this time."

He smiled. She really loved his smile. It was perfect except for the small chip in one of his front teeth that he'd gotten while playing soccer in grade school. But Becca thought the little imperfection just made him look more dashing.

They'd been together for as long as she could remember. Well, as far back as second grade. Anything before that was just a blur.

"So?" She leaned back and enjoyed his hands on her hips. "Where's my present?"

He smiled. "Not yet." He took her hand and started walking.

"Nick Becker, if this is some sort of trick." She was starting to get a little anxious. She didn't like surprises. Nick seemed to pick up on that and had always made a point of withholding things from her until the very last moment. Nick loved surprises, at least giving them.

He looked over his shoulder at her and smiled. She was thankful the moon was full on the warm summer night.

This fall they would be back in school and she hated knowing that they wouldn't get to spend as much time together as they had this summer.

2

When they walked into a clearing, she gasped. In the soft tall grass, a large blanket was spread out. A camp light sat in the middle and a picnic basket full of food was next to it.

"Happy birthday." He pulled her closer and kissed her, then pulled away quickly. "Here." He tugged on her hand until she sat down. "I've brought some of your favorites."

When he pulled out a bowl of his mother's mashed potatoes, she sighed. "My favorite."

"Mom's going to kill me when she finds out I stole this. She made this especially for her book club meeting tomorrow night." He smiled again. Then he turned and pulled out another bowl. "Here." He handed it to her.

When she peeled back the lid, she thought she'd died and gone to heaven. "Is this…"

"Chocolate pudding. I made it myself. It might be a little runny." He frowned.

"Oh, Nick." She laughed then set the bowl down and hugged him.

He cleared his throat and straightened his shoulders. "Now, shall we have a proper picnic?"

She giggled. "I'd love to."

They ate the little meal under the full moon as the warm summer breeze drifted around them. When all the food was gone, they lay back on the large pillows and watched the stars.

"I'm really thinking about joining the Army after school," he said absentmindedly, playing with the ends of her hair.

"Why?" She glanced at him. It was a conversation they'd had many times before. Since Nick was a year ahead of her in school, he was closer to leaving Pride,

Oregon, than she was. They'd talked about leaving town together after graduation, but more recently, he'd started talking about going into the military.

"Well, my father and my father's father were military men." She felt him shrug his shoulders. She could hear his heartbeat as her head rested against his chest.

Placing a hand on his stomach, she leaned up and looked down at him. "How long would you be gone?"

"Well, initially, two years." He reached up and brushed her hair away from her face. "I know I'm asking you to wait around for a year after graduation, but…"

She shook her head. "I'll wait." She smiled. "I'll always wait." She leaned down and placed a soft kiss on his lips. His hands went to her hips and held her closer.

"Becca?" he said against her lips. "I know you said you wanted to wait until you were sixteen." He looked at her and she felt that fluttery feeling she got every time they kissed. Then he glanced at his watch and smiled nervously. "Well, it is past midnight, so technically you're sixteen."

She smiled. "Nick, why do you think I agreed to come out here tonight?" She leaned down and kissed him again, trying to show him exactly what she felt. "Make love to me tonight for the first time, Nick."

His hands stilled on her hips, and she could have sworn she felt his heart jump in his chest. Or maybe it was her own heart that leaped.

They made love under the full moon, fumbling around, not knowing what they were doing. As the night went on, they grew to know each other's bodies and desires even better, bringing them closer than either of them could have ever imagined.

As Becca snuck back in her bedroom window and lay

down on her bed, she couldn't stop thinking about how wonderful the whole evening had been. Looking up at her bedroom ceiling, she kept playing her name over and over again, this time adding Nick's last name.

Becca Beatrice Becker. Mrs. Becca B. Becker. Mrs. Becca Becker. That sounded the best. She sighed and turned over in her bed, closed her eyes, and dreamed about the day she'd marry the man of her dreams.

# CHAPTER 1

*S*ix years later...

Pride, Oregon. What could Becca say about it. She had a love-hate relationship with the small town. Sometimes she felt trapped by it and the people who lived here. Other times she didn't think she could live another day without the help and support they provided.

Today was one of those days. It had been almost one year. One year ago, she'd gotten word that Nick, her one and only love, was gone forever.

She'd tried to keep herself busy ever since the day that he had jumped on the bus that would take him to basic training. After that, he'd joined the Special Forces along with his best friend, Sean.

The first year after he'd left had been filled with school and part-time work at her sister Sara's bakery. The second year, she'd gone to work full time helping her sister out with the business. Time had just flown by after that.

Until the day she'd gotten word that Nick was gone. Then everything had slowed down to a crawl. Every day it seemed like a chore to get out of bed, dress, and make her way down to the bakery. It took all her willpower just to greet the people as they entered the shop and to smile and act as if life was good.

For their part, everyone in town had made a point to be there for her. Every time she would burst into tears at the slightest thing, there was always someone there to hug and comfort her.

She'd never really felt like she'd been alone during her grieving, and she really hadn't. The whole town of Pride had been right there with her. They'd lost one of their own, and everyone was feeling the pain.

Sara was married now, and she'd moved out of their mother's house. And since their mother had sold her online accounting firm to a company in San Antonio, she was never really at home. Their mother spent half the year in Rio, where she'd bought a small condo on the beach.

The last time her mother had been home, she'd mentioned selling the house and living full time in the warmth.

"It's not like I can't come up here and visit once in a while. I mean, once I finally have some grandkids, I might be convinced to come up more often."

She'd looked at Sara and Allen when she'd said that. The couple had blushed a little and then Allen had smiled and said,

"We're working on it."

So most of the time, Becca was left alone in her child-hood home, feeling lonely.

Half a year after Nick had died, her mother had come home and packed up for the last time. The house had sold more quickly than even she had imagined. To be honest, the place was too big for just her. Besides, she was having a hard time keeping it up all by herself.

Her mother had arranged for her to move into the apartment over O'Neil's, the local grocery store, which happened to be right across the street from her sister's bakery, Sara's Nook.

Now her whole world consisted of two blocks. And it was two blocks only because she spent a lot of her time at the Golden Oar, the best—and only—restaurant in town.

Her sister was the chef and baker in the family, not her. Sara had shown her how to bake, and she spent almost every morning at work. Putting together ingredients or taking out warm bread and baked goods was easy, but when it came to feeding herself, she was clueless.

She knew how to heat up those little frozen meals she bought at Patty's downstairs. She'd tried to make chicken and rice once but had almost burned down the kitchen in the process.

It had taken her some time to get back in the groove of things after Nick's death. She'd thought about moving down to Rio with her mother but after finding out that her mother had a new live-in boyfriend, she'd decided against it. Besides, she'd never been out of Oregon before and the thought of hopping on a plane for the long trip scared her. Especially after losing Nick in a plane accident.

In the last year, she'd had more up days than down, thanks to the people in town and her sister. But she didn't think anything, or anyone could lift her spirits today. Today was the day that she had initially set for their wedding and the day Nick's best friend, Sean, was returning home from his tour.

The whole town was abuzz about the war hero

returning home. But the only thing that kept running through Becca's mind was that it should have been Nick. Not that she wished anything bad would happen to Sean. Just the opposite. Sean had always been there, a few steps behind Nick and her.

She was currently sitting in the back seat of Allen's truck as they headed up the hill to go to Sean's homecoming party. There was a fresh plate of Sara's brownies on her lap, which were still piping hot, warming her legs.

Spring was in full swing in Oregon, and she couldn't even look out her window to enjoy her favorite season of the year. Instead, her mind kept running back to the fact that Nick wasn't coming home. Ever.

She closed her eyes on a wave of pain, and her sister's voice broke into her dark thoughts.

"We'll stay only as long as you want. Okay?"

Becca's eyes opened, and she looked up to see Sara staring back at her. Concern dominated her dark brown eyes.

Becca had always been jealous of her sister's dark hair and brown eyes. She knew that Sara had felt the same about Becca's light hair and hazel eyes.

The two sisters were pretty much matched when it came to everything else, except Becca had a few inches on her older sister. Not that she was tall, but she did love to rub those two inches in Sara's face.

"I'll be fine," she said and looked back down at her hands. She wouldn't. She was lying. What she wanted to do was go back to her little apartment with the plate of brownies and watch movies all evening to help her get her mind off of things.

"I thought you and Sean used to be friends," Allen

asked, taking the last turn off the highway and driving his truck up the bumpy lane that led towards Sean's parents' house.

"Sure," she said, holding on as the truck hit a rut. She'd been up the drive plenty of times before. But it had been years since the last time.

"They need to fix this drive," Allen said under his breath.

"Maybe now that Sean is back in town, he'll help them. Patty was telling me that their house was falling into disrepair as well." Sara said, glancing out her window.

"Mr. Farrow had some health issues a few years back," Becca chimed in. "He's doing the best he can."

"I'm sure he is. I know when I ran into Mrs. Farrow the other day in the grocery store, she was looking forward to having Sean back. The woman was practically walking on air." Sara turned and looked at Becca.

Becca nodded and looked out the front window as they pulled into the large parking area in front of the old house. It did need some repair work. It could use a new coat of paint and all the bushes around the place had grown so tall, half of the house was invisible.

They parked in an available spot and when they got out, Becca noticed a few more cars driving up the driveway. She sighed. She knew almost everyone in town would show up, but she hoped to find a corner to hide in before too many had arrived.

"Here, I'll take that," Sara said, taking the tray of brownies from her. Instantly, Becca missed the warmth and the shield of holding something.

She followed her sister and brother-in-law up the stairs and through the open front door.

The room was already filled with voices and crowded with people.

Sean's parents stood just inside the door, greeting everyone as they arrived. Becca's heart skipped when she noticed the man in uniform standing next to them.

Pain shot through every pore of her body as their eyes locked. She couldn't stop the tears from coming as her eyes burned. She found it hard to breathe. Her eyes darted around the room, and she noticed everyone looking at her. Taking a step back, she felt the cool air and turned to rush out of the room.

Sean hated parties. Especially when he didn't think there was anything to celebrate. He was home, so what? It wasn't as if he had single- handedly taken down the enemy. Or saved a group of children from a burning building.

To top it all off, Nick was gone. Home wasn't home without his best friend and blood brother. Losing Nick was like losing part of himself. He'd known Nick since the cradle. His parents had practically raised the two boys as brothers. It helped that they lived within walking distance of one another and that their parents were also best friends.

It had been almost a year since Nick had died. He'd taken it hard, but being in the Special Forces, he hadn't really had time to mourn. Coming home and seeing the empty look on Nick's parent's faces had made reality sink in.

Then he'd seen Becca walk in his door. He'd watched

her eyes zero in on his and flood with such emotion, he'd felt like he'd been shot in the heart.

Becca's sister, Sara, and her new husband, Allen, had stepped in first. He was still shaking Sara's hand when Becca ran out.

"I'll go get—" Sara started to say.

"No." He tugged on her hand gently. "Let me."

When Sara nodded, Sean excused himself and stepped outside. He shivered. This weather was going to take some getting used to again. Six years of being overseas, and he'd grown accustomed to always sweating.

His eyes scanned the front yard and when he saw a branch move off to the side, he realized where she was going. Several other people were just driving up. He didn't want to be distracted, so he ducked behind a large bush and started to make his way to the tree line.

When he approached the old clubhouse Nick and he had built, he sighed, remembering all the good times they'd had in it: That time they'd spent all summer camped out in it when they were ten. Or the first time they'd invited girls to the little building so they could learn how to kiss.

He almost chuckled and then caught himself when he heard Becca crying inside. Becca had been Nick's first kiss.

Opening the door slowly, he ducked down to step inside. Had it always been this small? He remembered it being plenty big, back in the day.

Looking around, he was shocked to see that the little building was still in good shape. Then he saw Becca sitting in the corner. Her knees were up to her chest and her head was down.

Walking over, he sat on the old bench and picked her up off the dirt floor. She gasped a little, but when she noticed it was him, she collapsed into his chest and cried as he held her.

He hadn't had time since he'd come home to cry for his lost friend. But as he held Becca, the emotions leaked from his eyes as well. Memories played through his mind as his eyes moved around the room.

He could see Nick everywhere, and the more he looked, the more it hurt. Closing his eyes, he concentrated on trying to comfort Becca. He could only imagine what she'd gone through, staying in town and reliving memories of Nick everywhere, like he was doing now.

His heart broke a little as she cried. He tried to think of something else. Then his mind focused on how wonderful Nick had had it. Becca had stayed true to him all these years. She'd waited. He remembered all the times Nick would tell him about a call he'd had from her. About how they were moving ahead with their wedding plans. He remembered the last time he'd seen Nick. Nick had been so excited about going home to see Becca again. They had set the wedding date and Nick had even asked his advice on planning out the honeymoon.

"I'm sorry," Becca said against his chest, breaking into his thoughts.

"Don't be," he said, using the back of his sleeve to wipe away his own tears before she could see them.

She shook her head against his chest. "No, your parents must think—"

"They think you've had a hard time, just like we have," he interrupted. "My folks feel like they've lost a son."

She pulled back a little and looked up at him. Her eyes

were red along with the tip of her nose. She was still as beautiful as he remembered. He'd always been jealous of Nick and Becca's relationship. Not only because they had been so close, but because he'd always had a crush on his best friend's girl. Her caramel colored hair was a little longer than it had been the last time he'd seen her. Her face was a little thinner and he'd never realized how small she was before.

He wished he had a tissue to give her. Then he remembered there might still be a roll of toilet paper in the box under the bench. Reaching down, he felt for it while still holding her. He was in luck.

"Here." He handed her the roll. "It might be a little damp."

She shook her head and blew her nose and wiped her eyes. "It's fine, thank you."

"It looks like your folks didn't even step foot in here all this time." She looked around.

He nodded. "Yeah, they've neglected a lot around here."

"Nothing that can't be fixed." She started to scoot off his lap and he let her go. Instantly, he missed her warmth and how light she felt.

"Thank you." She glanced up at him.

"You've already said that." He smiled a little.

"No, for being here." She looked down at her hands. "I wouldn't have…" She shook her head. "It's hard for me to stop, once I get started."

He nodded, not knowing what to say.

"Are you going to be staying?" She glanced at him.

"Here?" He looked around.

"No." She chuckled a little. "At your folks' place."

"Oh." He thought about it. "I guess for a while."

She frowned a little. "You probably have plans to go somewhere more exciting now."

"More exciting?" He thought about it and shook his head no. "I've had a little too much excitement for one lifetime. I plan on staying in Pride." He had thought long and hard about it. Pride was home, even if it meant dealing with the pain of losing his best friend, he was going to stick it out. After all, this was the place he'd been dreaming about for the last six years.

She looked down at her hands again. "I hope you don't think that this was about you."

"This?" He wished she'd look back at him with those hazel eyes of hers. "Oh! No, not at all," he said when realization dawned on him.

"I just saw…" She looked back at him and her eyes connected with his. "I saw the uniform and…"

He nodded and pulled her closer. "I'm sorry. I should have changed, but my parents wanted…" He shook his head and wished he'd thought about the pain it would cause others to see him dressed like Nick would have been.

"Don't, it's okay." She nodded. "Everyone is so proud of you."

He didn't know what to say. They shouldn't be, not after the things he'd seen and done in the last six years. "Speaking of which. We'd better head back in. Do you think you're up for it?"

She pulled back and looked up at him, then nodded slowly.

"Good." He stood up and almost bumped his head on

the roof. "I don't remember this thing being this small before."

She chuckled. "I think the last time you were in here; you were almost a foot shorter." She smiled.

"Maybe." He frowned and held out his hand to help her up. "If you need anything…"

She nodded. "Thanks."

"Don't thank me." He frowned a little more. "Being around you helped me out, too."

He watched her eyebrows shoot up in question.

"I was feeling pretty bad in there." He nodded back towards the house as they stepped out of the fort. "I was dying for some air. So, thank you."

She smiled. "Anytime."

## CHAPTER 2

*W*hen they walked back into the party, Sara rushed over to her immediately.

"Are you okay?" She could see the worry in her sister's eyes.

"Yes, I'm fine." She was thankful when Sean stayed close to her. She felt his hand on her back and, somehow, it steadied her.

"Oh, honey." Sean's mother walked over to her. "Are you okay, Becca?"

Becca nodded and hugged the woman back. "I'm fine now." It was the truth. Usually, once she got the crying out, she felt better.

"Well, if you need anything." She hugged her again.

"Thanks." Becca looked around the room and noticed Nick's parents sitting at the table next to Sean's father. "I'd better go…" She nodded to the table.

Sean's mother nodded. "I know that they would love to see you." She smiled.

When Becca walked over to the table, Nick's parents

stood and hugged her. She'd thought that she was done with crying, but every time she saw the couple, she started back up.

"Come over here; sit with us for a while," his mother, Lynn, said. "We've missed seeing you around. It's all Phillip's fault really." She smiled at her husband.

Her husband chuckled a little. "Trying to watch my waist." He patted his belly. "Every time we go into the bakery to see you, we have to have some of your sister's delicious treats. I was gaining five pounds every time we stepped foot in the bakery's doors."

Becca laughed.

"I don't know how you work there and still look like you do," Lynn said.

"Too much sugar gives me a headache." Becca sat next to the woman and was happy when Sean settled next to her.

"We are just so proud of this boy," Phillip said, patting Sean on the back.

"It seems like just yesterday that Sean and Nick were in diapers," Lynn said, smiling a little. "Where does the time go?" She sighed, and Becca could see a little sadness in her eyes.

"So, what kind of job will you be looking for, now that you've decided to stick around?" Phillip asked Sean.

Sean looked a little lost. "I hadn't really thought about it. I was going to spend some time helping my folks out around here, first."

"That's good," Sean's father piped in. "Since I broke my leg a few years back, I haven't been able to keep the place up myself."

Sean nodded. "After that, I'll see what happens." He looked out the window like he was thinking about it.

"I know Robert has an opening down at the office," Lynn said absentmindedly. Robert Brogan had been sheriff of Pride for years. He was also a regular at Sara's Nook. He liked his raspberry-filled donuts and vanilla latte every morning. The last time he'd been in, he'd been complaining about being short staffed.

"Working for the sheriff?" Sean seemed to think about it. "That wouldn't be such a bad job, I suppose."

She nodded her head and smiled. "Of course, there's always teaching football at the high school. Johnathan Princeton was in the bakery the other day with a broken leg." She smiled. "He'll be out this whole season, so I know the school will be looking for someone to run drills during the summer."

"Hmm, football." Sean frowned a little. "Dealing with a bunch of moody teenagers. I think I had enough of that in high school and the forces."

Everyone laughed.

"You could always join the Coast Guard," Allen said from behind her. Becca turned and glared at him. It wasn't a bad idea, but he was always pushing everyone she knew to join up.

"There's a new subdivision being built on the other side of town, near the sports complex. You could get hired on as a contractor," Nick's father said.

For the next ten minutes, more and more ideas were presented to Sean. Becca could see him becoming a little overwhelmed with everyone being so concerned about his next move.

Finally, when she could, she stepped in and changed the subject to the weather.

"I think I'm going to go mingle." Sean stood up a few minutes later and excused himself. His eyes zeroed in on hers as his eyebrows shot up in question. It was clear that he was asking if she wanted to go with him.

"I'll just go find my sister," she said, looking around. Allen took her place at the table as she and Sean made their way towards the back of the house where most of the noise was coming from.

She should have known it would be coming from the Jordan clan. The entire back room was filled with the large family.

"I thought that this is where the party would be," Sean said, stepping in and shaking Todd's hand. Todd was the oldest, but Lacey, his petite younger sister, was the rowdiest.

"Don't mind us," Lacey said, smiling. We were just celebrating your return home without you."

Everyone chuckled. The next few minutes were filled with Sean greeting everyone in the room.

Becca stood off to the side, talking with Todd's wife, Megan, as she held their youngest, Susannah, who was fast asleep. Even with all the noise going on, the little girl's blonde head rested against her mother's shoulder.

"She can sleep through anything." Megan smiled. "I suppose it helps that she tries to keep up with her big brother and sister."

Becca smiled and rubbed the back of her finger against the girl's chubby cheeks. Becca had babysat for the Jordan's on several occasions, as well as for Lacey and Aaron.

But after she'd started working with her sister full time, she'd passed on the babysitting to Cara, her younger neighbor.

"Are you okay?" Megan asked quietly. Becca nodded her head and looked up into the woman's blue eyes, seeing concern and compassion there.

"I'll be okay." Becca and Megan had talked on several occasions after Nick had died. Megan had lost her only brother several years back and Becca knew that Megan understood the pain she'd gone through.

"Well, if you need anything." Megan touched her arm.

Becca smiled. "It's weird having him back." She nodded to Sean. "I mean, seeing him without Nick."

Megan smiled. "From what I hear, the two were pretty much inseparable."

Becca nodded. "Trust me, you didn't see one of them without the other being a few feet behind." She chuckled. "It did get a little awkward when Nick and I started officially dating."

Megan smiled. "Kind of like our Matthew and his cousin Conner, Iian and Allison's boy." She nodded to the kids' corner where two little boys around the same age were huddled together. "Conner is two years younger, but they look the same age." Megan shook her head. "That kid is going to be tall."

Becca smiled. "Of course, it helps that both of his parents are giants." She nodded over to where Iian and Allison stood, talking with Sean. She was a little surprised to see Sean using sign language to communicate with Iian, who was deaf. She hadn't known that Sean knew the language. Of course, she'd been too focused on Nick back in the day to ever really notice Sean.

23

She watched him now. He was a lot taller than Nick had been. Of course, her memories could be wrong. It seemed the more she tried to hold onto memories of Nick, the more she forgot. She could remember the color of his eyes, the way his smile made her melt, and how he felt next to her. But she had a hard time remembering his voice, the richness of his laugh, and even how he smelled. It was those things that always made her sad.

Sean laughed a little at something Iian had said, bringing her attention back to him. He had a nice laugh. Hearing it reminded her of the times she'd found Nick and he huddled together in the fort out back, laughing at comic books.

She couldn't stop herself from smiling.

"He's a good-looking man," Megan said, smiling at her. "I'm sure he's looking forward to getting on with his life around here." Becca looked over at Megan and nodded.

"Well, I think I'm going to go find a quiet place to lay this little one down." She ran a hand over the sleeping baby's back. "Talk to you later. Remember, if you need someone to talk to…"

Becca nodded and watched Megan disappear. When she turned, she almost bumped into Lacey.

"Oh!"

"Sorry." Lacey smiled. "I have a habit of sneaking up on people."

Becca smiled. Lacey was one of her favorite people in town. When the woman had been pregnant with her second child, George, she'd come into the bakery almost on a daily basis, sometimes twice a day. When she'd gotten a little too big, she'd sent her husband.

Looking down at the smaller woman now, you would have never guessed how big she'd gotten during that time.

"How's it going down at the bakery?"

"Good." Becca sighed. "Of course, we lost our best patron when you had George."

Lacey chuckled. "I swear it was all that boy's fault." She glanced over at the child playing in the corner with a few other kids. "He still has a sweet tooth," Lacey whispered.

Becca laughed.

"How are you doing?" Lacey looked back towards her.

"Fine. I'm fine." Becca smiled, but she knew why everyone was asking. It was so hard to keep up the facade. What she wanted was some more fresh air.

"I'm going to step out, get some fresh air." She nodded towards the back doors.

When Becca stepped out on the back deck, she inwardly sighed when she noticed she wasn't alone. Several of the older people sat out there, talking under the awning.

She didn't feel like talking anymore, especially since everyone seemed so concerned about her. It was getting old having everyone ask her how she was doing.

How did they think she was doing? The love of her life was gone. Just gone. She slipped down the side steps and walked towards the front of the house. Maybe there she could have a moment to herself.

Working at one of the busiest places in town meant that you knew everyone. Not just little circles, like most people did, but everyone.

Usually, seeing people and chatting with them helped

her stay distracted. But today was different. Today, she wanted to be left alone.

She found a small bench along the side of the house and sat down. She didn't know how long she sat out there alone, but when her sister came and got her, she was ready to leave.

"I'm sorry we stayed so long," Sara said, opening the truck door for her. "Allen got to talking." She smiled over at her husband.

"Right." He smiled back.

"It's okay. I enjoyed myself," she lied.

"Right," Sara said, looking back at her.

"Well, I didn't *not* enjoy it." She frowned a little and looked out the window as they drove off. She hadn't even told anyone good-bye, but she wasn't up to it. Besides, it wasn't as if she wasn't going to be seeing everyone soon anyway.

Most everyone in Pride stepped through the doors of Sara's Nook sooner or later.

Sean had such a busy week working on his parent's house that he hadn't had time to swing by and talk to Becca again. He'd missed seeing her after he'd watched her disappear out the back door. She must have snuck out and then left with her sister and brother-in-law. He'd been too busy listening to all the job ideas from everyone who'd attended his party to notice her go. He was starting to question if his parents had put everyone up to it.

He'd been putting off giving Becca the box of Nick's stuff. It wasn't that he was scared of what Becca would feel, just that once the box was out of his hands, he'd feel that loss all over again for his friend.

But it had been over a week since he'd seen her at the party, and he knew it was time to make a trip into town and stop by her sister's bakery.

When he drove up, he saw the closed sign in the window and frowned. Glancing at his watch, he saw it was after three. He'd meant to get here earlier in the day, but he'd been too busy chopping down the rhododendron bushes in front of his parents' house.

At least he'd finally gotten the place looking like a house instead of a jungle. But now that the house was visible, he could see it needed a fresh coat of paint as well as new shingles on the roof.

Sighing, he was about to pull out of the parking spot when he glanced over at the grocery store and saw Becca standing in line to check out.

Jumping out, he dashed across the street in the light rain that had caused him to stop all the outside work for the day.

When he walked into the grocery store, he noticed that Patty O'Neil was checking Becca out. Instantly, he wished he'd waited outside for her to come out.

"Well, look at who finally comes back," Patty said loudly. "Bout time you made it in here." She smiled and waved him over. When he stepped close to her, she gave him a big hug.

"It's good to see you again, Patty." He hugged her back. The woman had gotten smaller since the last time he'd seen her. "Are you on some sort of miracle diet? I swear you're half the woman you used to be." He smiled at her.

27

She laughed and patted her hair back into place. "Well, listen to you, Mr. Smooth Talker." She winked at Becca, who smiled. "I have been going down to the Boys and Girls Club, working out with a bunch of other ladies. They do aerobic swimming classes there now."

"Well, you look wonderful." And the truth was, she did. She not only looked half the size, but almost half the age.

"I was just telling Becca, here, about how we're meeting three times a week now." She turned back and continued to scan Becca's items.

He noticed there were a great deal of frozen dinner boxes in her cart and frowned a little.

"Well, what brings you down our way?" Patty asked as she swiped Becca's credit card.

He nodded to Becca. "I was hoping the bakery was still open."

Becca shook her head. "We close at three. We're open again at five tomorrow."

"Five? In the morning?" He frowned. "Since I've been back, I've made a promise to myself that I wouldn't step foot out of bed before six." He smiled.

"I bet you're enjoying it," Patty said, handing Becca back her card and the receipt.

Sean took two of Becca's bags. "I'll help you out. See you later, Patty."

"Such a gentleman." Patty smiled and waved them off as she started checking out the next person in line.

"You don't have to…" Becca started, frowning at him as she grabbed up the other bag.

"It's no problem." He pushed open the door and held it

wide for her to step through. He looked around. "Where's your car?"

"Over there." She nodded down the street. "But, I'm not going to it. I'm up here now." She nodded towards the stairs.

He glanced up at the apartment above the store. "You're living there? What happened to your house?"

"My mother sold it and moved to Rio full time."

He frowned as he followed her up the stairs. He couldn't imagine living on his own, going through everything she had all by herself.

At the top of the stairs, she turned and reached out for the bags.

"I'll help you inside. I have something for you." He watched her eyes sadden. She nodded her head and opened the door.

The apartment was nicer than he'd expected. The view from the second story windows was breathtaking. The buildings in front were lower, and you could see the water from there.

"I bet that's a killer view on a clear day." He set her bags down on the counter and nodded towards the windows.

"One of the reasons I've stayed here." She sighed and started removing boxes of frozen meals from the bags. She placed them in her freezer as he watched.

"Is that all you eat?" He nodded to the meals.

"Hmm," she said as she loaded up her freezer.

"That stuff can't be good for you." He reached over and took a box from her. "I mean, just look at all this stuff they put in here." He started reading off the ingredients.

She leaned back and crossed her arms over her chest and watched him.

"It's these or starve." She took the box from him and set it in the freezer with the rest.

He shook his head. "I can teach you how to cook. There are a few basic meals you should know how to make." He walked over and opened her cupboards. They were pretty much bare.

"What are you doing?" She stood back as he opened her refrigerator.

"Looking for something to eat."

She chuckled. "Are you hungry?"

He stopped and looked over at her. "Yeah, aren't you?"

She shook her head. "It's three thirty in the afternoon."

He shrugged his shoulders and pulled out the chicken she'd just put in the fridge. "It will be an hour before this is done." He held up the chicken. "I may have to run downstairs for a few more things." He frowned and set the chicken on her countertop. "Don't move."

He didn't even give her time to respond. Instead, he headed back downstairs and spent the next fifteen minutes shopping for items he would need to make his Italian chicken.

Patty may have a small store, but she prided herself on carrying some of the best organic vegetables and fruits around. He could get lost in the variety. He'd missed shopping and cooking while he'd been away.

As he carried two more full bags up the stairs, he opened the door without knocking and smiled when Becca was still standing in the kitchen, looking down at the chicken.

"What are you doing?" she asked, stepping aside.

"Making us dinner," he said, pulling items from the bags and setting what he would need on the large cutting board she had sitting out.

She leaned against the large island and shook her head. "Why?"

He stopped, turned, and looked at her. "Because I'm hungry and the thought of you eating frozen dinners up here alone drives me mad."

She nodded her head slowly and then walked around and sat at a bar stool.

"Oh, no." He shook his head and moved over and took her shoulders and walked her back into the kitchen. "You're going to help."

"I can't cook. I'll burn—"

He chuckled. "Can you cut up vegetables without cutting off a digit?"

She nodded.

"Good, then grab a knife and cut these up."

"All of them?" Her eyes got huge when she saw the large pile of vegetables in front of her.

## CHAPTER 3

$\mathcal{B}$ecca had to admit, chopping vegetables gave her a little satisfaction. She occasionally glanced over to see what Sean was doing. He was making some sort of sauce and putting it and the chicken in one of the large glass pans her sister had given her. When she was done with all the vegetables, he scooped them into the pan with the chicken and placed it all in her oven.

"There. Now we wait." He glanced down at his watch. "Plenty of time to have a beer." From her fridge, he pulled out two cans that he'd brought downstairs. Handing one to her, he popped his open. "You know; this is one of the things I missed the most." He took a deep drink of his beer.

"Beer?" She frowned down at her drink. She liked beer. The fact that he'd bought her favorite brand had her a little unnerved, especially since she remembered it had been Nick's favorite too.

"No, cooking." He took her hand and walked her to the sofa. "Sit." He nodded and sat after she had.

"You enjoy cooking?" She shifted and got a little more comfortable.

He nodded. "I know, right?" He chuckled. "Nick always made fun of me about it." He shook his head and took another drink of beer. "That was until he tasted what I'm making us now."

"It's that good?" She chuckled when he nodded and gave her a lopsided smile.

"Yeah, I perfected it in high school Home-Ec classes. One of the main reasons Skyler started dating me."

Becca stilled when she heard the name. "How is Skyler? I haven't heard from her in a while."

He shrugged his shoulders and took another drink. Then his eyes went to her windows as the rain started coming down harder.

"We broke things off a while back," he said. She couldn't gauge his mood since his eyes were focused on the rain.

"I'm sorry," she said and set her half-empty beer down.

He shook his head. "Don't be. I should never have proposed to her."

Her eyebrows shot up. "Why not?"

He chuckled a little and glanced sideways at her. "You know why."

For a moment, Becca's heart skipped, not fully under-standing him.

"She could never be faithful to anyone. I thought that she would settle down after graduation." He shook his head and took another sip of his beer. "From the sound of things, she actually got wilder."

Becca nodded. "I've heard. I'm sorry."

He shrugged his shoulders and set his beer down. "I

have something for you." He frowned. "It's out in my car." He glanced towards the windows again.

"You can get it when the rain lets up." She leaned back and tucked her legs under herself.

"I like your place." He nodded around. "How long have you been here?"

"Almost six months."

"Do you like living right in town?"

She shrugged her shoulders. "It has its perks. I can walk to work and the grocery store." She smiled. "Saves on gas. Plus, Patty gives me a great deal on the rent."

"I'll need to look for a place of my own." He shook his head. "Not that I don't like staying with my folks, but it's time." He leaned back and propped his foot on his knee.

"There are a few apartments for rent in the Meadows." She frowned when he cringed. "They fixed the places up last year. Remodeled over half of them. They're really nice now."

"I might swing by." He sighed. "But to be honest, I was hoping to buy a house. I have some money saved up and, with a VA loan for the rest, I think I could find something I could fix up."

She reached for her beer again. "There are a lot of older places for sale in town. Or were you thinking of something out by your folks' place?"

He shook his head and watched her. "I hadn't thought about it that far."

"I know what you mean. After..." She took another sip just to swallow the pain. "After Nick, I didn't know what I was going to do. I can't imagine coming back after what you've been through."

His eyes went back to her windows as the rain continued. "I should have planned more. Maybe I should have stayed in the military."

She set her drink down and leaned back again. "Is that what you want?"

His eyes moved to hers and it took a while for him to shake his head no. "I don't know what I want for now. Does that make me bad?"

She shook her head. "No! Absolutely not. You have your whole life ahead of you now. Take your time and don't let anyone pressure you into making a decision too soon."

His lips curled up a little. When his hand reached out to brush the tips of her hair, she held her breath.

"Thanks." He surprised her by quickly standing up. "I'd better check the food."

When he moved into the kitchen, she closed her eyes and tried to steady her breathing. She didn't know why she had jumped at his feather-light touch.

"Almost done," he said from behind her. "The rain has let up some; I'll go grab the box from my car." She heard the door shut behind him.

She nodded, not taking her eyes off the large windows. The sky was still dark and gray, but she could tell that the rain had let up a little. Her place was starting to smell wonderful.

For a moment, she let her mind wander to what it would be like to be with another man. Someone like Sean. She'd never been with anyone other than Nick and didn't think she'd know how to act if someone showed signs of being attracted to her.

She'd never been good at flirting. There had been no need with Nick. She knew life had to go on, and in the last few months, she'd started believing that there was someone else out there for her.

She didn't think Nick would want her to continue living life mourning him. After all, she was only twenty-two. Way too young to write romance and falling in love off her list forever.

Sean opened the door and stepped inside. He shook his head, letting the raindrops fall from his dark hair. As she watched him, she couldn't stop herself from comparing him to Nick.

Nick had been smaller and had lighter hair. His blue eyes had been one of her favorite features. Looking over at Sean, she saw his dark eyes watching her.

"Are you okay?" he asked as he set a large box on her table.

She nodded her head slightly as he removed his jacket. His shirt had gotten a little wet from the rain and her eyes went to the toned muscles that ran down his arms.

Nick had never had those, either. Of course, the last time she'd seen him, they had been kids, really. She sighed, not realizing her eyes were still on Sean's arms and chest.

"If you want, we can wait and open this after we eat."

She glanced up at his eyes and for a moment, she forgot what he was talking about. Then she looked down at the large box and frowned.

Nick's things were in there. Pain shot through her. She nodded her head. She didn't think she'd be able to eat after seeing what was in there.

"If you want to set the table, I'll get everything else ready," Sean said, motioning towards the table.

She stood up and walked over to the kitchen without a

word. Her eyes kept moving back to the box like something was going to jump out of it.

She was thankful when he moved it to her coffee table.

When they sat down at the table, she had to admit, the food not only smelled good, it looked great. He'd arranged everything on the plates and the chicken, noodles, and vegetables looked more like art than food.

"Well?" He smiled over at her. "Are you going to try it?"

She smiled. "I was just thinking that if I took a picture of this, I could hang it on my wall and enjoy it longer."

He smiled. "Presentation is part of the package."

She picked up her fork and took a bite. Her eyes closed, and she tried not to moan at the wonderful tastes.

It was pure torture watching Becca eat. He didn't know what had caused him to wonder what it would be like to kiss her. But once he started, he couldn't stop.

His eyes took in everything. How she looked at him. How her tongue darted out to lick the sauce from her lips. He was quickly losing his mind and there was nothing he could do to stop it.

He tried to focus on his dinner, but the fact was, he'd lost his appetite—for food, anyway.

"I thought you were hungry?" she asked, glancing at him. He nodded and tried to refocus on the meal. Even the cold beer did little to calm him.

Once both of their plates were empty, she stood up and took them to the sink. "That was the best meal I've had in a long time. Well…" She glanced back at him. "Since the last time I ate the Golden Oar, that is." She smiled.

"I'm glad you liked it. You've got to start eating better. Those frozen meals will kill you." He shook his head. She frowned a little. "I can teach you if you like?"

She chuckled. "My sister tried." She leaned back against the countertop. "Even my mother gave up on trying."

He smiled and carried his empty beer over and set it in the trash can. He watched her eyes zero in on the box he'd set on her coffee table.

"I can stick around if you want?"

Her eyes went back to his quickly. "I'd like that. I know it's probably childish of me…"

He shook his head and walked over to her, taking her shoulders in his hands. "Some things you shouldn't do alone."

She nodded and when her eyes met his, he thought he saw confusion.

Then she stepped away and walked over to sit on the sofa again. He followed her and pulled the box closer to them.

When she lifted the lid, she sighed a little. Sean hadn't looked inside the box. It had taken most of his willpower to hold onto Nick's stuff for over a year. This box had been marked with Becca's name and had been found at the bottom of Nick's footlocker.

She pulled out a Special Forces T-shirt, held it up to her face, and took a deep breath.

"I had forgotten…" She closed her eyes and took another breath. "I'd forgotten what he smelled like." Her tears started to fall and knew there would probably be more before she was done.

"I always remembered him smelling like gym class." He chuckled as she smiled.

"After you two would play basketball during the summer…" She smiled. "I swear I never knew boys could stink so much." She chuckled as he smiled. Then she took another smell of his shirt and set it down.

When she pulled out a framed picture of Nick and her, her eyes watered again. "You took this picture," she said, nodding at it.

He remembered. They had driven down to Haystack beach and spent the day collecting shells and digging for clams. Nick's arm was thrown around Becca's shoulders. They had huge smiles on their faces. Sean could hardly remember ever being that happy, except when he'd been with them.

"That was a great day." His smile felt forced as he felt his heart dive a little. Nick was gone. It still felt like a bad dream.

"What is this?" She held up a sealed brown envelope.

He shook his head. "I didn't go through his things."

She set the picture down on the coffee table and opened the envelope. Her frown grew and for a moment, he began to worry.

"This…" She shook her head. "This can't be right."

"What?" He moved closer to her. "What is it?"

"It looks like an online itinerary with prepaid passes." She held up two passes as she looked over a bundle of papers stapled together.

"For what?" He took the passes from her.

"A cruise," she said under her breath. "Nick bought

passage and made travel plans for our honeymoon." She glanced up at him through teary eyes.

He shook his head. "He'd mentioned something about it…" He took the paperwork from her and read over it.

"A cruise from Florida to the Bahamas with a four-night stay at the SLS Lux in Nassau. There are even prepaid airline passes here." He held up the paperwork that had all the information."

"When did he do all this?" She closed her eyes and he could tell she was fighting the pain. He set the paperwork down and pulled her close.

"He asked where I thought he should take you for a honeymoon." He laughed and closed his eyes on the memory. "I told him that he needed to give you an adventure." He smiled as he held her while she cried.

"I'll never see him again. I'll never get married," she said, crying against his chest. "I'm going to die all alone."

He shushed her and rubbed his hand over her hair, trying to comfort her as she cried. He pulled her closer when he felt her body go lax. Her feet were tucked up underneath her and her arms had wrapped around his waist. His shirt was wet where her tears had fallen against his chest. He didn't mind. He leaned his head back and closed his eyes and remembered the last time he'd seen his friend.

## CHAPTER 4

*B*ecca felt stiff and sore. Her fingers tingled and when she tried to move them, pain shot up her arms.

"Sorry," Sean mumbled, shocking her. He moved a little, releasing her hands from behind his back. "Are your hands asleep?" He sat up a little and took her hands in his and began rubbing them.

"Ouch." She pulled them away as the blood flooded back into them.

"No, trust me, this works." He continued to rub her hands quickly. Her eyes moved to him and she stopped focusing on everything but his face. It was a lot darker in her living room now, so half of his face was shadowed. There was a full night's growth of hair on his face, making him look darker, sexier.

She blinked a few times, trying to get her eyes to adjust. She remembered what had happened now. She'd cried against his chest until she'd fallen asleep. She looked down at his shirt and noticed that the spot she'd cried against was still a little damp.

"There, is that better?"

She looked up at his eyes again and nodded. She'd forgotten the pain since his warm hands still held hers.

His eyes moved to hers and she felt him tense a little. "Becca?" He whispered her name.

"I'm sorry," she said at the same time.

He shook his head and blinked a few times. "Don't be."

She looked down at their joined hands and then closed her eyes when he released her hands.

"If you want…" Her eyes flew back to his as he spoke and for a moment, she knew exactly what she wanted. "I can see about getting a refund on this trip."

Her heart fell a little. She quickly shook her head no. "I don't know what I want to do just yet." She leaned back. "I'm sorry about keeping you here."

He lifted her chin up until she looked him in the eyes. "Don't be. I was glad I was here. I enjoyed dinner, being with you again."

She nodded, then glanced over at her clock and gasped. "It's four o'clock."

He wiped his hands over his face and then looked down at his watch. "So, it is."

"I'm going to be late." She started to get up; his hand went to her arm, holding her still.

"Late? You go to work at four?"

She nodded. "Four-thirty."

He shook his head. "Too early, if you ask me."

She smiled. "If you want to stick around, I can promise you some hot sticky buns. Sara makes the best

44

and they're so good when they're fresh from the oven."

She heard his stomach growl. "Looks like you have a direct line to my stomach." He chuckled. "Sounds like its mind is already made up."

She laughed. "I'll just go shower. Feel free to rest some more." She nodded towards the sofa.

When she stood up, she realized he'd toed off his shoes at some point last night. She'd lie on top of him all night, with her hands trapped underneath him. She couldn't remember sleeping so well in the last year.

As she showered, she couldn't get her mind off of how Sean had felt against her. He'd been warm, and just resting her head against those muscles of his had been a treat.

It had been years since she'd been that close to a man. She liked it, and it made her pause when she realized she wanted more.

When she walked out of her bedroom dressed for work, she frowned a little when she saw Sean reading over the paperwork from Nick's box.

She would have never imagined that Nick would do something so romantic for their honeymoon.

"These are non-refundable prepaid passes." Sean frowned up at her. "And they expire in about a month."

She looked down at him, not knowing what to say.

"I'm sure if I call, they might make an exception, due to the circumstances."

She shook her head again. "No." Something inside her didn't want to cancel the trip. She didn't know if she wanted to go on the cruise, but she wasn't sure she didn't want to go, either. She wanted more time to think about it before she decided.

"I have to go." She glanced out the window and could see that her sister was already next door. "Sara will be needing me. You can stay here,"—she looked around—"until we open the doors at five, then come on over."

He nodded. "Thanks, I'll lock your apartment door."

She chuckled. "This is Pride. There's no need to lock up. Remember?"

He frowned and shook his head. "It's hard for my mind to get back into the swing of small towns."

She smiled. "You'll get used to it again." She walked to the door and grabbed her umbrella. "Thanks again for dinner and…" She left the rest hanging. He nodded his head.

"Anytime." His smile warmed her to her toes.

She walked out before she said or did something stupid.

When she walked in the back door of the bakery, Sara stopped what she was doing and smiled at her.

"So, Sean, huh?"

Becca stopped and almost tripped. "What?" How did her sister know?

Sara laughed and moved to the little window that looked out to the front of the store. Then she pointed, and Becca could see Sean still sitting on her sofa, looking down at the picture of her and Nick.

"It wasn't like that." She sighed as she watched him looking at the picture, sitting on her sofa.

"Too bad," Sara said and walked back over to finish rolling her dough. "I always liked him."

Becca turned and looked at her sister. "But for some reason, you never thought that Nick was good enough for me."

"He wasn't." Sara glanced up at her. "Don't you know by now? No one is ever going to be good enough for my little sister." She sighed and looked down at her flour-covered hands. "But Nick did eventually grow on me."

Becca crossed her arms over her chest and leaned against the wall.

Sara looked up at her. "He did. I would have been proud of you if you two had married."

Becca nodded. "Sean is just a friend. He's always been just a friend."

"Does he know that?" Sara asked.

Becca shrugged her shoulders and glanced over her shoulder again at Sean. He'd moved from the sofa and was now standing by her windows, looking out. She knew he wasn't looking in her direction, but she still moved away from the little window, just in case.

By the time Becca opened the doors, she was feeling a little surer of herself. Helping Sara bake always cleared her mind. Even though Sara had two full-time bakers, Becca always helped out when she could.

For the most part, Becca worked in the front of the store. She usually loved dealing with customers, but there were days she wished she didn't have to.

When Sean walked in a few minutes after she'd unlocked the front doors, she smiled.

"I've saved you the biggest sticky bun. Want some coffee with that?"

He smiled and nodded. "Black. None of that fancy stuff either, just good ol' fashioned coffee."

"Really?" She glanced at him as she poured him a cup. "Didn't they have lattes or cappuccinos overseas?"

He chuckled. "They did, I just never could stand

them." He sat down at one of the little tables. She set his coffee and the hot bun in front of him. "Do you have a moment to sit with me?" He nodded to the chair.

She glanced around and noticed Sara had stepped out front to help the next customers. Sara winked at her and she frowned a little as she sat down.

"These are the best thing I've had in years," he said, breaking into her thoughts. She smiled a little as she watched him take another bite.

"I told you so." She leaned back.

"I think you should go," he said after taking a sip of his coffee.

"I'm sorry?" She frowned a little.

"On the cruise." He looked up at her. "I think you should go. It's what Nick would have wanted."

She closed her eyes and sighed. "I was trying to talk myself out of it, but I agree with you."

He nodded and smiled then started to take another bite.

"Go with me," she blurted out, causing him to choke on his coffee. She quickly moved behind him and started pounding on his back.

"Easy," she said when he finally started breathing normally again.

He took a deep breath. "You want me to go on what would have been your honeymoon?"

She frowned and looked down at her hands. "I hadn't thought it through. Not really."

His hand reached across the table and took hers. "Go, enjoy yourself."

She shook her head. "How could I? All by myself?" She closed her eyes.

"Take your sister or a friend."

Becca glanced over at Sara and frowned. "Sara would never leave the shop for that long." Then she looked back at Sean. "You *are* a friend. Probably the closest one I have besides Nick."

He sighed and looked down at their joined hands.

"I'll go, if you will go with me, as my friend," she said, standing her ground.

She'd never been anywhere outside of Oregon, and here was an opportunity to fly to Florida and then travel to the Bahamas on a cruise ship. The idea scared her, but for some reason, she knew that if Sean went with her, she would enjoy herself and not spend the whole trip thinking about Nick.

Sean was shocked. He couldn't go with Becca on Nick's honeymoon cruise. But he didn't want her to miss out on the opportunity herself.

The fact that Nick would have wanted her to go ate at him. He sat in silence as he finished his sticky bun. Becca had rushed to help another customer, leaving him alone at the table, deep in his thoughts.

"You should go." He looked up and saw Sara standing next to him. "It's a small room and I'm very good at eavesdropping."

"What about you?" he asked as she poured him more coffee.

She looked around and when she noticed her sister was engrossed in helping someone, dipped her head down. "I can't. Don't tell anyone yet, but we're expecting. I couldn't even handle a cruise on a normal day, let alone

49

now." She chuckled lightly.

"Congratulations," he said quickly, but she hushed him and glanced around again.

"Thanks." She smiled. "You should go. I think Nick would have loved to have his two best friends enjoy themselves."

He frowned down into his coffee mug. "I think it would be weird."

Sara laughed. "Life is weird. Things are thrown at us and sometimes we have to go with the flow. Go with the flow on this. Tell Becca you'll go. Have a wonderful time and watch over my sister for me."

He looked up into Sara's eyes and when he saw honest concern, he nodded.

"Good. Now, do you want another sticky bun? This one's on me." She smiled.

He left the bakery after putting away both sticky buns and enough coffee that he felt like he sloshed back to his car. He hadn't told Becca yet that he'd agreed to go along.

When he walked into his parents' house, his folks were sitting around the table eating breakfast.

Since his father's accident, his mother had him on a strict diet. The veggie omelets looked and smelled wonderful. If he hadn't just shoved in a bunch of sugar and starch, he would have enjoyed sitting down with them. Instead, he headed upstairs to shower.

By the time he was clean and dressed, he'd pretty much talked himself out of going on the cruise with Becca. When he walked downstairs, his mother stopped him from leaving.

"What's this about you going on a cruise with Becca Lander?"

He almost missed the last step of the stairs and landed on his face.

"Who told you that?"

His mother crossed her arms over her chest. "Well, I would have hoped to hear the news from my son, but Sara called me and convinced me to convince you not to back out."

He frowned down at his mother.

"You should go," she said. "Seriously, go."

"Wouldn't it be weird?"

"No. You two have been friends almost as long as you and Nick were. Besides, she could use the company, and taking a trip for pleasure would do you some good, help you clear your head. Maybe then you can decide on something for your future. Now, since Sara also mentioned that you'd had two of her sticky buns"—his mother's smile grew— "you can go outside with your father and help chop up some wood. Winter comes quickly around here and that wood pile doesn't get magically stacked."

He groaned, wishing he'd thought about catching a few more hours of sleep before he'd come downstairs. But he headed outside because he didn't want his father working in the sun all by himself.

By the time he left his parents' place, freshly showered again, he was questioning himself all over again. Chopping wood had done little to help him make a decision. He'd tried to focus all his attention on deciding his future. He didn't like it that people were discussing his future behind his back. He knew Pride was small and the great people in town loved to talk about other people's lives.

As he drove back towards Becca's, he started thinking about her again. Maybe he should go with her. He'd never been on a boat for relaxation before, and sandy beaches and warm water *were* sounding pretty good. By the time he parked outside of her place, he'd made up his mind.

## CHAPTER 5

*T*here were days that Becca wished she didn't have to climb the stairs back up to her apartment after work. She sighed as her hand rested on the railing and she looked up the long flight.

"That rough of a day, huh?" She jumped at Sean's voice behind her, then smiled as she leaned back on the railing and nodded to him. He shook his head. "After getting home, I had to chop two whole cords of wood for my dad." He sighed and rubbed his shoulder with his other hand. "My arms haven't hurt this bad since boot camp."

She smiled at him. "When you've been on your feet since four thirty in the morning, you'd do anything to stay off them for the rest of the night."

He nodded and then surprised her as he swung her up in his arms and started up the stairs. "What are you doing?" She gasped and looked around quickly. It was too late; they'd been seen by at least two people in town. Closing her eyes, she groaned.

"Just helping you out." He chuckled.

"I thought you said your arms hurt," she said, keeping her eyes closed.

"They do, but you're as light as a feather." He stopped at the top of the stairs and set her down. "See, wasn't that better than climbing them yourself?"

She nodded her head and pushed open her door. "Well, come on in." She waved to the women who had stopped in the grocery store parking lot to watch the show. "Great, now that's going to be all over town by dinnertime."

He chuckled. "Speaking of which, my mother heard it from your sister that I was going on the cruise with you." He walked over and sat on the sofa.

"What?" She shut her door and leaned against it. "I didn't think you'd decided yet."

He turned and looked at her. "Didn't your sister tell you?"

She shook her head, and he moaned as he shut his eyes. "Leave it to women to spread the word to everyone except the one person that matters most."

Her heart skipped. "Are you going?"

He looked at her again and nodded. "If you still want me to."

She nodded and felt her palms getting sweaty. She wiped them on her jeans after she hung her jacket up.

"Would you like to stay for dinner? I've got…"

He chuckled, stopping her. "I know what you have. What about heading to the Golden Oar? I haven't been back there since I've been home, and I'm dying to see what new things Iian has on the menu."

"Sounds good. Let me just change." She looked down at her flour-splattered shirt and work pants.

"Sure, take your time. I'm just starving here." He chuckled.

"If I remember correctly, you're always hungry." She smiled as he nodded, and then she walked out of the room to change.

They walked into the Golden Oar less than an hour later. It was still a little early for the dinner rush, but the place was already filling up. It was the first nice evening after three days of rain, and most people in town were looking to get out on the town.

They were shown to a table near the wall of windows that overlooked the water.

"I've always loved this place," Sean said, sitting back in his chair. "The food, the atmosphere, the art." He nodded up to the half-naked mermaid.

Becca laughed just as the waitress walked up to take their orders.

When they were alone again, she tilted her head and looked at him. "You're pretty good at cooking. Have you ever thought about opening your own place?"

He laughed. "I can cook a few dishes, but make no mistake, I'm no master like Iian Jordan." He nodded towards the man in question.

Iian had been head chief of the Golden Oar for almost as long as anyone could remember. Even in his teens, he'd worked in the kitchens. He was simply a master at making food look good and taste great.

"Speaking of which…" She turned back towards him. "I didn't know you knew sign language."

His eyebrows shot up as he looked at her. "There's a lot about me that you don't know. Your eyes were always glued to Nick." He smiled. "Not that it was a bad thing; just that your kind of let life pass you by for a while there."

She frowned a little. "I did? What do you mean?"

He shrugged his shoulders. "I guess we all notice what we want in life."

She thought about it for a moment. "Like how you thought about Skyler?"

He sobered a little. "Yeah. I wanted her to be something that she could never be."

"What was that?" She leaned forward a little.

He looked her right in the eyes and said, "Like you."

Sean felt like kicking himself for letting that slip. He'd been caught up in the conversation. He hadn't thought of how his words would sound when spoken out loud.

"I…" He shook his head. "I mean; how loyal you were to Nick." He looked back down at his hands.

She smiled and nodded her head. "It's okay, I understand. Skyler wasn't the best girlfriend."

He released his breath and nodded.

"Why did you propose to her in the first place?" she asked after their drinks were delivered.

He shrugged his shoulders and looked down at his hands. "Nick had just proposed to you, and Skyler was very set on following your lead. She was very determined to marry. You know, she actually wanted to get married before I left?"

She shook her head. "Skyler got what Skyler wanted." She sighed. "I'm sorry."

He shrugged his shoulders again. "I'm just glad it ended."

"About that." She frowned a little and he started to worry. "Does Skyler know? I mean, have you officially broken it off with her?"

He nodded. "During the last of the three Skype calls we had over the last six years."

"Three? Only three?" Becca shook her head.

"Yeah. It's one of the reasons I knew it was over a long time ago." He shook his head, remembering how Nick had always gotten excited for the once or twice a month calls he would get from Becca. "Nick was always filling me in about your calls, and he mentioned a few times how you'd told him about Skyler."

"I'm sorry." She looked down at her glass. He reached over and took her hand.

"Don't be. I was glad when it ended. It was almost as if I'd been freed from a prison."

"Was your relationship with her that bad?"

He shook his head, not wanting to let go of her hand, so he held on a moment longer. "No, we'd only been dating my senior year." He sighed and looked out the window. Then he turned back to her. "Why did you ask if Skyler knew it was over?"

She winced a little and looked out the large windows at the water. "She stopped by the bakery today. Shortly after you left."

"And?" He felt a headache coming on.

"She was going on as if you two were still an item." She shook her head. "I don't even think she realizes you're back in town. Funny, everyone in town knows but her."

57

"She knows." He frowned remembering the call he'd gotten from her the first night he was home. He'd even told her not to show up to his party and was thankful she hadn't.

Just then, Iian stopped by their table to make sure everything was okay. Sean talked with him for a while in sign language. Iian didn't speak much, but since he'd married and become a father, he'd started talking more and more. The man was an excellent lip reader.

"I hear you two are going on a trip soon," he said.

Becca had just taken a drink of her water and started coughing. Sean nodded after making sure she was okay. "Yeah, I'm going to call and arrange it all tomorrow."

"Well, I know you two will have a great time. Allison and I went on a cruise down to Mexico for our honeymoon." He smiled and sighed. "Our anniversary is coming up." He rubbed his chin with his hand. "Might be time for another one. I hear the Disney cruises are nice for parents."

Sean smiled and nodded. After Iian left them alone again, Becca leaned forward and whispered.

"Do you think the whole town knows?"

He chuckled. "Probably so." Then he frowned a little. "Does it bother you?"

He watched a small crease form between her eyebrows. "No, not really. I've never been one to worry about gossip."

"Then what?" He leaned a little closer to her.

"Do you think that everyone will think that we're sleeping together?"

He didn't know how to respond, so he shrugged his shoulders a little.

"Not that it matters." She frowned as she looked down at the table.

"If it bothers you, I can stay…"

"Don't you dare." Her eyes flew to his. "You can't cancel on me." She shook her head. "I don't know if I would have the guts to go through with it."

"It's just a trip." He frowned a little.

"It's the first time I'll be leaving the US. Oregon for that matter."

"You've really never been outside of Oregon?"

She shook her head no.

He reached over and took her hand when he saw the sadness in her eyes.

"Don't worry. I'll go. Traveling is not as scary as you might think." He smiled to reassure her.

"I don't know. Just knowing all the plane accidents that happen each year…"

Frowning, he remembered when he'd heard about Nick's flight and how it had skidded off the runway in Munich. "Becca." He waited until she looked him in the eyes. "Nothing like that is going to happen. It was a fluke. You're safer flying than driving a car. So they say." When he squeezed her hand, she nodded.

Just then, the waitress walked up to deliver their food, and he dropped her hand. Instantly, he felt the loss.

It was hard to concentrate the rest of the evening. He kept stealing glances at Becca. Their conversation flowed, as it always had between them, but he couldn't stop himself from feeling a little on edge.

Maybe it was the fact that the sun was setting out their window, casting some of the most beautiful colors he could ever remember. Or, maybe it was just the company he was in.

She'd changed from her work clothes and was

wearing a sundress that hugged her in all the right places. The color almost matched her eyes and with the dying sunlight streaming through the window, he was quickly realizing he was a romantic underneath his tough exterior.

Poems and songs kept popping into his head. Every time he looked at her, he imagined them being together. It was so hard for him to put all his desires aside. He knew it was probably just the long sexual hiatus that was driving him mad.

But as he drove her back to her apartment, he was silently wishing she'd ask him upstairs.

His heart skipped as they pulled into the parking lot at the grocery store. Parking next to her car, he turned in time to see her look up at her apartment nervously.

"What?" he asked.

She looked over at him and frowned. "Nothing." She shook her head. "It's just…" She sighed. "Did you really mean what you said about Skyler?"

He chuckled. "I said a lot about Skyler tonight."

"About how you wished she was more like me?"

He nodded, waiting for her to continue.

"I'd always wanted to be more like her." She sighed and rested back in the seat. "I know it's bad, but I always wished I'd had the guts to do some of the things she's done in the last couple years. Do you know that she went to Paris? Twice?" She sighed.

"Traveling doesn't make you a good person."

"Oh, I know that, but to get out, explore new places. See places that most people only dream about." She sighed.

He frowned. "I went to almost every country during

my time with the Special Forces." He frowned as he remembered almost every trip. "Still, I prefer Pride."

"It's probably different. I mean, you were there for official business. But to travel for pleasure..." She glanced at him and then shook her head quickly. "I have that paperwork upstairs."

"Paperwork?" He frowned.

She giggled. "You said you were going to call and schedule the trip. You might need the receipt and pass information."

"Oh." He nodded. "I'll come up if that's okay?"

She nodded and smiled at him. He kept telling himself he'd run up, get the paperwork, and leave. Simple. He was trying to convince himself that was why she asked him up. Not to sit on her sofa and kiss her until the sun came up.

Shaking his head, he got out and rushed around to open her door for her. He forgot to move aside after he'd opened the door, and she ended up bumping solidly into his chest. Her hands went up between them and his went to her hips to steady himself. When he looked down at her, she was smiling up at him and he felt his breath leave him.

"It's been a while since I've had a man do that," she said softly.

He blinked a few times, trying to remember how to breathe, how to speak.

She smiled and chuckled a little. "You know, open a car door for me."

"Oh," he said again and felt his fingers tighten on her soft hips.

"Sean?" she said, leaning a little closer to him.

"Mmm?" His eyes were glued to her lips. Wishing. Wanting.

"People are staring." She chuckled.

His eyes moved from her lips to her eyes, and he could see that she was looking off towards the parking lot. Glancing over, he noticed Amber and Luke smiling at them.

"Evening," Luke called out.

Sean nodded his head. He and Luke used to be buddies in school.

"How's it going?" Sean dropped his hands from Becca's hips and took a big step back.

"Can't complain," Luke said, loading a bag of groceries into the back of their car. "I was glad to hear that you're back in town."

Sean nodded. "Might be heading out again for a while." He nodded to Becca.

"Yeah, heard about that too." He chuckled and pointed to Amber behind her back. Sean got the hint and nodded. "Well, when you get back for good, let me know. I've got some news," he said as he loaded up the last bag.

"Will do." Sean watched as Luke opened the door for Amber and they drove off.

"News?" Becca asked. "I wonder if they're pregnant?" She sighed and leaned back against his car.

He turned to her and frowned. "What makes you jump to that conclusion?"

She chuckled. "Didn't you see what was in those bags?" She nodded to their car as they drove up the hill.

"No." He frowned.

"There was enough ice cream to feed an army." She smiled and started walking towards the stairs.

"So, maybe they're having a party?"

She shook her head. "The whole town would know if

they were having a party. Besides, Amber has been out sick the last two days."

"Now how do you know that?" He watched her open her door.

"Small towns. Besides, I have a gift for these kinds of things."

"Oh really?" He chuckled, thinking of the secret he was keeping for her sister.

"Sure." She set her bag down and walked over to the sofa and sat down. "Like, I bet you didn't know that my sister is pregnant." She smiled over at him and he felt his jaw drop.

Then he walked towards her with a smile. "Actually, I did."

This time it was her jaw that dropped.

"Liar." She crossed her arms over her chest and kicked her sandals off.

He shook his head and sat next to her. "She confided in me just yesterday." He smiled. "The question is; how do you know? She told me it was a secret."

"Oh, it still is. I can just tell. For starters…" She leaned back and tucked her feet up underneath her. "She stopped trying all the food she was making."

He shrugged his shoulders. "So, maybe she's just watching her weight."

She chuckled and shook her head. "I mean; she won't even touch a bite. And when I asked her to try some frosting I'd made, she shook her head and rushed to the bathroom."

He nodded and chuckled. "I guess morning sickness is a telltale sign."

Becca nodded and looked off to the dark window.

"Things are changing so fast." She sighed.

"Like what?" He reached over and absentmindedly played with the tips of her hair.

"Sara and Allen, Luke and Amber, and you." She looked over at him.

"Me?" His fingers stilled in her hair and he watched her bite her bottom lip as her eyes locked with his.

# CHAPTER 6

*S*he nodded slowly. "You, being here." He looked at her questioningly. "Not here, here." She looked around. "I mean, home."

Why did it seem like whenever he got this close to her, her brain and mouth stopped working?

"Change is good." It almost came out as a whisper. She nodded a little. "Isn't it a good thing that I'm here?"

She nodded a little too quickly and he smiled. Her eyes were glued to his mouth and she couldn't stop herself from wondering what those lips would feel like pressed against her own.

His eyes were sparkling with mischief, and she had the funny feeling that he had meant here, here. Not just in town.

"Becca?" She loved hearing him say her name. His voice was rich and sexy and made her knees feel weak.

She hadn't even really known that his hand was in her hair, not until he pulled her closer until they were a breath away.

"This is probably a mistake," he said, just before his lips glided over hers.

She couldn't have imagined the kiss if she'd spent years trying. His lips were softer and warmer than she'd envisioned. His hand was in her hair, holding her close as his other traveled to her hip. She felt his nails dig in a little. Her own fingers traveled up his arms until she gripped his shoulders.

Her eyes closed on a moan as his tongue darted out and licked her closed lips. She opened for him and tilted her head and felt her breath hitch at the taste of him.

She lost track of time and place as her head spun and her world became only about him and taking her next breath.

When he pulled back, it took her a minute to realize why he was frowning at the table. Her phone was ringing, and she hadn't even noticed the noise over the sound of her heart beating in her ears.

"I'd better…" He got off the sofa quickly and started walking towards the door. She frowned down at her coffee table and noticed the paperwork sitting underneath her phone.

"Sean?" She jumped up from the sofa and raced towards him. He turned quickly back towards her, his hand on the doorknob. "The papers." She handed them to him as he frowned and nodded to her.

He didn't say anything as he walked out. When the door shut behind him, she leaned back against it and sighed. Then her phone started ringing again and she raced to answer it.

"Hello?"

"Oh, there you are, Becca. I was beginning to wonder

if I'd better send out the troops to make sure you were okay." Her mother chuckled.

"Hi, Mother." She walked to the front windows and watched Sean's car disappear up the hill. She sighed and closed her eyes and mind to one of the best kisses she'd ever had.

"Hello?" Her mother said a little louder. "Are you there? I think we have a bad connection."

"Sorry." She walked back over to the sofa and plopped down on it. "I'm here. What's going on?"

"Well, I was just telling you that Paulo was going to be coming with me on this trip to meet you, girls."

"Hmmm." She nodded. "That will be nice." She tucked her feet under herself and tossed the blanket that sat on the back of her sofa over herself. For some reason, she was chilled. As she talked to her mother, she tried to convince herself that it had nothing to do with the fact that Sean's warmth had seared her, and she desperately missed it.

"So, what's this I hear about you running off with Sean Farrow?" Becca almost choked on air. "So, the rumors are true." Her mother giggled as she continued to cough. Becca could just imagine her rubbing her hands together, plotting out the wedding.

"I am not running off with Sean," she finally said when she'd gotten her breath back.

"Well, of course, you aren't." She could hear the smile in her mother's tone. "I'm sure you two are just going to take a friendly cruise to the Bahamas and stay in one of the fanciest hotels in Nassau." She sighed knowing her mother wasn't done. "Oh, and stay in the same room, too."

Becca's eyes flew open. "We are not…" She stopped herself and thought about it. Were they staying in the same room? She couldn't imagine Nick getting two suites. Either on the cruise or at the hotel.

"I see by your silence that you hadn't thought that far ahead. Well, I have, dear. You say the word and I'll pay for an extra suite for you."

"No, Mother. That won't be necessary. After all, Sean and I are just friends." The thought of the kiss that her mother's phone call had interrupted flashed through her mind. She closed her eyes again and rested her head back on the sofa.

"It's okay, honey. I think everyone in town will agree with me that it's okay." Her mother sighed. "I know you. You're a lot like I am. I beat myself up for years after your father left. I didn't want to date or even just go out with friends. Of course, my situation is a lot different since I had to deal with a lying, cheating…Sorry." Her mother let out a large breath. "Anyway. You loved Nick. Nick loved you. It was tragic, losing him. But don't do what I did by locking yourself away. Go. Get out. You're so young. Enjoy yourself. If something happens between you, roll with it."

Becca wished her mother would just stop talking, but she continued for almost another five minutes.

"Listen, Mom, it's been a very long day."

"Okay, think on what I said. Promise me."

"Yes. Have you talked to Sara yet?"

"I just got off the phone with her before I called you. Why?"

"Did she tell you anything?" Becca bit her bottom lip.

"Like?" Her mother dragged out the word.

"Nothing. It's not for me…"

"Becca, what is going...No, never mind. I'm hanging up now and calling her right back. Love you, sweetie."

"Love you too."

Becca watched the clock and estimated it would take less than ten minutes for her sister to call her.

Just enough time for some dessert. She walked into the kitchen and pulled out a container of ice cream. Since it was officially gossip night, she might as well enjoy being stuck on the phone.

By the time she had half the container emptied, her phone was ringing again.

"How did you know?" Sara sounded a little winded.

Becca laughed. "You can't get anything past me."

"We were going to tell you this weekend." Sara sounded a little disappointed.

"I've known for a couple days. Sean tells me he even knows. I wonder how long it will take to spread through town."

Sara sighed. "Oh, knowing our mother, it's already going around. No doubt there will be a lot more customers in the bakery tomorrow morning, all wanting to congratulate Allen and me."

"Good. Then you can work out front." Becca took another bite of ice cream. "Oh, that reminds me, I think Luke and Amber are in the same way."

"What? Who told you?"

Becca laughed. "The two bags full of ice cream I just witnessed them loading into their car."

"Hmm," Sara said. "How wonderful. After all, we did get married just a few weeks after they did. It would be so nice to have our kids grow up together." She could hear the wistfulness in her sister's voice.

"Don't go planning playdates yet. It's just a hunch."

"What are you eating?" Sara asked after a moment of silence.

Becca looked down. "Blue Bunny Rocky Road."

"Great. Now I want some ice cream."

"So, get some," she said, taking another bite.

"We don't have any." Her sister sounded like she was whining.

"You have a man. Make him go get you some."

"He's still at work. They are having problems with one of their teachers." She sighed. "I do have a sister that lives above the town's only grocery store."

Becca laughed. "No way. I've spent all day on my feet. These puppies are staying right where they are." She wiggled them under the blanket and smiled.

"But…Just think of your niece or nephew."

Becca smiled. "When he or she gets here, I'll make sure to spoil him or her rotten. But, until then, morning comes awful early and my boss doesn't like it when I'm late."

Sara laughed. "I guess I can call Allen and have him pick some up on the way home." She sighed. "How did things go tonight with Sean?"

"Oh, no." Becca shook her head and finished off the ice cream. "My love life, or lack of one, is not open for discussion at this time."

"But…" Sara was whining again. "I'm bored."

Becca laughed. "Watch TV. I'm going to go take a hot bath and read a book until I fall asleep."

"What book are you reading?"

"'Night, Sara." Becca listened to her sister sigh and then hung up.

❄

What had he done? The whole drive home he kept asking himself that question as images of Nick's face flooded his mind. Of course, he hadn't thought of Nick when he'd been kissing Becca. No, his mind had been flooded with wonderful visions of her, wonderful smells, and of course the sweet way she'd tasted on his lips.

Shaking his head, he pulled into his drive and groaned out loud when he saw Skyler's car sitting behind his dad's truck.

Before he could get out of his car, she was walking towards him. She hadn't changed much in six years. Her hair was still very blonde and styled pretty much the same as it had been in school. She dressed and acted like she was still in school, as well.

He supposed many people would find the short shirts and tight tops to be a big turn on.

"Well, there you are. I thought I was going to have to wait around all night." She wrapped her arms around his waist and the smell of alcohol hit him full force. He could see that she wasn't drunk, which was a blessing because he didn't want to have to call a cab for her or, worse, drive her home himself. For some reason, the thought of being in a car with Skyler for five minutes made his stomach uneasy.

"What are you doing here?" He unwrapped her arms from his body.

"What? Can't a girl come and see her man whenever she gets an itch?" She tried to lean towards him, but he stopped her.

"I'm not your man. Remember?" He gripped her hands in his to hold her still.

Her eyes grew large. "You didn't really mean all that. It was just a little fight." She giggled and sighed. "Besides, now that you're home, things will go back to the way they were. You'll see." She wiggled her hands until he released her. "There." She smiled and rubbed her chest against his arm. "Now, why don't we go somewhere where we can be alone?" She purred.

"It's not going to work, Skyler. I meant what I said. We're through and have been for a long time." He moved her aside, so he could shut his car door. "I'm going in to get some rest." He turned back to her. "Go home." He walked into the house. Both of his parents sat in the living room, looking like they'd been desperately trying not to eavesdrop.

He almost laughed at the innocent faces they were trying to make.

"Evening, son," his father said from behind the newspaper.

"Don't worry, she's gone." He chuckled when he saw his mother sigh with relief. "I don't know why she just won't take a hint."

His mother got up and started walking towards him. "Some women are just—"

"Stupid," his father blurted out causing everyone to chuckle.

"Now—" A loud crash interrupted his mother's next words.

By the time they made it outside, Skyler's taillights had disappeared down the drive. He walked over to his shattered front windshield.

"Well, now, that's a shame," his father said next to him. "Want me to call Robert?"

Sean shook his head. "Won't do her any good. Besides, maybe now she's gotten it out of her system and we can move on." He turned to his mother. "Don't worry, my windshield was cracked and needed to be replaced anyway." He walked over to her and put his arm around her shoulders. Had she always been this small and petite? He shook his head. The woman had always been a giant in his mind. He felt her vibrating and for a moment, though she would burst into tears.

"That bitch." He looked down at her and saw that it wasn't sadness, but anger. "Who does she think she is? Coming onto our land, destroying our property? I'm going to go in and call the sheriff."

"Now, Lori, it's not our place. If Sean doesn't want to press charges, then we need to leave it up to him."

His mother turned on his father. "What's to stop that crazy woman from setting the house on fire?" She waved her hands around and walked over to point a finger at her husband's chest. "I told you that girl was trouble from the get-go."

His father chuckled a little. "Yes, you did. You can sure spot 'em."

"What does that mean?" She put her hands on her hips and glared at his father.

He shook his head and walked over to wrap his arms around her. "Just that you have excellent taste." He leaned down and kissed her.

"I married you, didn't I?" She wrapped her arms around his shoulders and kissed him back.

Sean had grown up seeing his parents' affection, but he

still cringed every time they kissed in front of him. Especially when they continue to kiss for a long period of time.

"Aww!" he groaned and turned away. "Do you have to do that in front of me?"

He heard his folks chuckling.

"You do what you feel is right, son." His mother walked over and gave him a peck on the cheek. Then she pinched it. "But stay away from that one. She's crazy."

He smiled and nodded. "Yeah, that message was received loud and clear."

The next morning, he made a few phone calls and arranged everything for the trip. The hardest part had been switching the tickets from Nick's name over to his own. But after sending the airline a copy of Nick's death certificate, they were all set.

Their flight from Portland to Miami left in two days. From there they would hop on the cruise ship for three days to Nassau where they had one of the best suites at the SLS Lux. They would stay four nights there before hopping on another cruise home.

He'd never in his life imagined spending that much time just relaxing. In the last six years, he'd always been on the go. Sure, he had R and R every now and then. A night here or there. He'd even gotten to enjoy a few weekends in Berlin. But nothing like this. Especially when he thought about taking the time with Becca.

He tried not to think about the kiss, but his mind kept playing it over and over in his head. He knew he had one more stop to make and even though he'd talked to Sean's folks over the phone, he needed to do this last thing in person.

When he drove up to their place, his sweaty palms let

him know just how nervous he was. Wiping his hands on his jeans, he knocked on the door.

Lynn, Nick's mother, answered. She was a short woman, shorter than his own mother. Where his mother had rich dark hair, Lynn was a blonde. Although he doubted it was natural. She looked young and healthy, but the sadness in her blue eyes told him everything.

"Sean, you know you don't have to knock." She smiled and waved him in.

"Yes, I know." He stepped in and nodded to Phillip, Nick's father. Phillip had been in bad health recently, or so his parents had informed him. But just like his mother was doing for his father, Lynn had him on a special diet, and Sean could tell it was doing the man some good.

"Well, hello, Sean. What brings you over here on this fine day?" Phillip stood and shook his hand.

"I wanted a chance to talk to you both in person. Before word got out."

"Is this about the trip?" Lynn asked, motioning for him to sit down on the sofa.

He nodded and sat.

"We've already heard," Lynn said, sitting across from him. "We're happy you're going with Becca. She shouldn't go alone."

He looked down at his hands. They were still sweaty, and he wished the knot in his throat would go away.

"Well?" Phillip leaned forward a little and looked at him. "Did you get everything switched over alright?" He nodded again. "Then, what is it?"

He looked up at Nick's father and felt like bursting into tears. "I guess I just wanted to know that it was okay? That we're okay?"

Nick's parents looked at him for a long time. "Son, we are always okay with whatever you plan on doing," Nick's father said.

"Honey, you're like a son to us. We love you as much as we loved Nick. You have our blessing in whatever you want to do in life. We're so proud of you for helping Becca out. We know it's been so hard on the two of you, just as it has on us this last year," Lynn said. Her husband reached over and took her hand in his and nodded.

"I…" He looked down at his hands again. "I feel like I'm betraying Nick somehow." His voice sounded far away.

"Oh, honey. You shouldn't. Nick loved you like a brother. He wouldn't want us sitting around wasting our lives feeling bad all the time. We didn't raise him like that, and I know that's what he'd want for you now. You're so young. So much of your life is ahead of you."

He nodded, knowing in his heart that what she was saying was true. He'd been telling himself the same thing for almost a year.

"Go, have a wonderful time. Be young. Be alive." She smiled as a tear fell down her cheek. "Nick would have wanted it."

He stood up quickly and pulled her up into his arms as his tears fell.

CHAPTER 7

ow could flour cause such a mess? It wasn't as if she was new to the whole working in a bakery thing. She knew that adding the flour to a mix too quickly was bad, but she'd been so preoccupied that she'd lost track of how fast she was pouring it into the mixer.

Now, she was not only covered in flour, but it was caked into her hair since she'd shown up to work with it still damp.

She was in the bathroom, trying to pull chunks of flour out of her hair when her sister burst in and started getting sick.

Becca rushed over to her and rubbed her back as she hunched over the toilet.

"I'm sorry," Sara said when she was finally able to sit up. "It's all Josie's fault." She leaned back against the wall and closed her eyes.

"What did she do now?" Becca smiled. Josie was Sara's best friend and business partner.

"She made me..."—Sara held her stomach— "drink

some nasty tea. She told me it would help the morning sickness."

Becca chuckled. "She's probably getting back at you since she had to hear about the pregnancy from Patty."

Sara shook her head and closed her eyes. "No, at first I think it worked." She sighed and leaned her head against the wall. "Then, I was feeling a little too confident and tried to have a nibble of a scone."

Becca shook her head. "What are you going to do without me while I'm gone?"

Sara's eyes flew open. "You are coming back. You better come back."

Becca chuckled. "Of course. What? Did you think I'd run off with Sean and never be seen or heard from again?"

Sara shrugged her shoulders, then stood up and walked over to the sink to rinse her mouth.

"I mean…Sean and I?" Becca laughed.

"What's wrong with you and Sean?"

Becca stopped and looked at her sister. "Well, for starters…" Her mind went completely blank.

"See!" Sara pointed towards her. "You can't even think of one reason you two shouldn't be together."

Becca shook her head, trying to clear it.

"I mean; you're attracted to each other. The whole town knows that by now." Sara smiled and dried her hands.

"No, they don't!" That snapped Becca back a step.

Sara chuckled and nodded. "It's like you're on fire when he's around. Your face gets flushed and your eyes go dreamy." Sara made a funny face and held her hands up to her chin and sighed.

"Oh, please." Becca yanked opened the bathroom door

and then realized she still had flour in her hair. "I'm running home to shower before we open the doors."

Sara smiled. "I kind of like your new look." She tugged on her hair and they both laughed as a plume of flour rose from her hair.

Three hours after the doors opened, Becca saw Sean's car park across the street and her heart skipped a beat. Then she noticed the windshield and worry set in.

When he walked into the bakery, she rushed over to him. "Did you get in an accident?" She looked him over for any sign of injuries. He looked fine, but he didn't answer; he just frowned down at her.

"Well?" She stopped right in front of him. "What happened to your car? It looks like a brick flew through it. Were you driving when that happened?"

He shook his head and smiled a little. "A brick did go through it, but I was in the house at the moment."

Becca put her hands on her hips and waited. When he didn't say anything more, she sighed. "Sean Thomas Farrow, are you going to tell me what happened? Or do I have to call your mother?"

He chuckled. "Okay, fine." Then his smile fell away. "But I get a cinnamon roll and a cup of coffee first."

"Fine." She walked behind the counter to get his order.

She set the plate and cup in front of him, sat across from him, and waited until he took a bite and a sip. Then she cleared her throat and gave him an impatient look.

He smiled a little. "Skyler paid me a visit last night."

Becca felt herself vibrating with anger. "She did that?"

He nodded as he took another bite.

Becca looked off towards his car. "Did you call—"

79

"No, and I'm not going to. Hopefully, she'll take it as we're even."

"Even?" Becca looked at him. "Even? What are you talking about? You haven't done anything to her." She leaned forward. "She's the one…" She looked around and noticed that several other people sitting in the small dining area had stopped talking. She shook her head. "Later." She sighed. "Stop by for dinner?"

He smiled again, and she felt her heart skip. "Six okay?"

She nodded and got up to help a customer who had just come in.

"I'll stop by the Golden Oar and pick up some pizza on my way over."

She smiled down at him. "Did you think I was going to cook?" Becca laughed and shook her head as she walked off to help the new customer.

When he arrived at her door a few minutes before six, his arms full of pizza and dessert from the Golden Oar, he couldn't explain the nerves that raced through him.

He'd eaten at her place before, but for some reason, this felt different.

He was glad when she met him at the door.

"Wow, that's huge." She laughed and took the bag full of desserts from the top of the pizza box.

"Yeah, it's called a King Pizza. Iian's new addition."

Becca laughed and shook his head. "I'll just bet he could plow through one of these by himself. How the man eats like he does and looks the way he does…" She shook his head. "Do you know, I watched him wolf down half a dozen cinnamon crumb muffins in one sitting?" She set the bag down on the countertop and turned to him. Her smile fell away a little. "Sean, about earlier…"

His mind went to their kiss the night before. Instantly his heart fell a little. Did she regret it? Did she not enjoy it? Oh, god! Why did he feel like a teenager around her?

"About what you said at the bakery. You haven't done anything wrong to Skyler." She shook her head. "You don't owe her anything. She's the one that ran around, cheating on you. She lied and told everyone all sorts of stories about you."

He walked closer to her and set the pizza down. "I just meant…" He sighed. "I shouldn't have proposed to her. I feel like I wasted so much of her time. She should have gone off and married a man who could handle everything that is Skyler."

Becca laughed. "No such man exists."

He chuckled and took a step closer to her. When he noticed her breath hitch, he smiled a little.

"About last night."

She swallowed and nodded.

"About this…" His hand went to her face. "Are you okay…"

She smiled and nodded slowly. "I think so. I mean, I don't know." She closed her eyes as he rested his forehead against hers. "I hadn't expected it."

"Neither did I. Trust me." He pulled back and looked at her. "How about some pizza? I'm starved." He couldn't have cared less about the pizza right then, but he needed a moment to calm down. She looked so fresh tonight. She must have just stepped out of the shower since her hair was still damp. It smelled like strawberries and he wanted to lick her skin to see if she tasted as good as she smelled.

When she smiled and nodded, it took all his willpower to take a step back.

"There's a game on if you want to watch it and eat in the living room."

He chuckled. "I thought you'd never ask. If I remember correctly, you're a huge Denver fan."

She smiled and nodded. "And you're a Seattle fan."

He laughed. "Maybe if Oregon ever gets a baseball team, we can both root for the same team."

She chuckled. "Maybe, someday."

He smiled and took a slice of pie. He found it so easy to talk to her as they watched the game. Even though neither of their favorite teams was playing, they still enjoyed cheering and arguing over plays. It was just like old times.

By the time the dessert was gone, he felt so relaxed and right about his decision to go on the cruise with her.

"So, we really leave the day after tomorrow?" She sighed and leaned back on the sofa.

He nodded. "If you have your passport."

She smiled. "I got it a few years back. I was going to surprise Nick when he was in Mexico." She frowned a little. "But then they moved him to Germany instead." She sighed.

"I remember. He was really bummed about not being so close to you."

"It must have been hard for you guys. To be so far away from home. From everyone you loved."

He nodded. "We had our unit. They pretty much

became our family." He smiled. "There was never a dull moment, that's for sure."

"Were you two stationed together a lot? Nick never could tell me much."

He nodded. "Still can't tell you much, but, yes. For the most part, we were together. Except for that last year." He frowned. "I was called to Asia and he stayed in Munich."

"Nick never really told me what you did. I know you were both Special Forces."

He nodded and frowned as he looked down at his hands. "Have you ever heard of combat divers?"

"Like in water? No. I thought the Navy took care of everything water?"

He shook his head. "Almost every branch of the military has a team of combat divers. They're used for lots of different reasons. Underwater demolition, special warfare, ops, explosive disposals." He watched her face pale a little. "We were mainly salvage and infiltration. We spent the first year and a half in training in Key West." Becca tucked her feet up underneath her. Reaching over, he played with the ends of her hair. It was completely dry now and looked like honey in the soft light. "We went to UOS, Underwater Operations School. It's funny, both Nick and I passed with flying colors." He chuckled remembering how shocked they were that they were both really good at the same thing. Fate. That's what they had called it. "So, we officially became frogmen and because we worked well together, they shipped us everywhere as a team. Divers need to be able to trust who they dive with. We worked, and it made sense to keep us together."

"What did you do? I mean, I get that you were divers, but…"

He shook his head. "You'd be surprised at how many situations call for maritime infiltration."

She smiled a little. "You make it sound like a James Bond movie."

He chuckled. "Some days it felt like it." His smile faltered a little. "Others, it was just a job."

"Did Nick enjoy it?"

When he looked at her, he couldn't really read the emotion behind her eyes. He nodded. "Loved every minute of it. Actually, when he heard about the Coast Guard setting up camp in town, he was thrilled about it. He even thought about getting a job being a trainer after his time was done."

She smiled. "He would have been a good teacher."

He frowned a little and looked down at his hands. Nick would have been an excellent teacher. But Sean didn't think he had it in him to do that kind of job. Didn't think he had the patience.

"What about you?" Her question threw him off. "Did you enjoy it?"

He nodded slowly. "At first. Maybe I was riding on Nick's coattails because, after a while, it lost some of its shine."

She nodded. "I know what you mean."

He waited and when she didn't continue, he probed a little. "What has lost its shine for you?"

She looked up at him and he felt tightness in his chest. Her eyes were mesmerizing, so beautiful. He wondered why he would ever look away.

"It was fun at first, working for my sister at the bakery. But lately." She sighed and shook her head.

"So many people have been asking me what I want to

do since I returned home. I'd hate to sound like them, but what does Becca want?"

She smiled. "Don't let anyone rush you."

He smiled and shook his head. "Don't worry; I'm setting my own pace."

"Good." She sighed. "Becca wants to teach history."

His eyebrows shot up.

"Oh, don't give me that look." She laughed. "I'd be great at it. Young kids of course. I don't think I want to deal with teenagers, either."

He smiled. "Of course."

She frowned at him. "What does that mean?"

He laughed. "I remember what you were like as a teen. No wonder you want to avoid dealing with it again."

She reached over and punched him lightly on the shoulder. He faked being hurt and she smiled.

"Why don't you?" He reached out and played with her hair again. It was quickly becoming a pleasurable habit.

She shrugged her shoulders. "I haven't had the time to go to school. Or the money." She sighed. "I've been saving up, you know, for the wedding. And after Nick died...I thought I would use it for school, but I guess time just got away from me."

"Maybe when we get back, you can look into it."

She nodded. "I think it's time." She smiled at him. Maybe he didn't know what it was he wanted to do with his future, but at that moment, he knew that whatever it was, he wanted her to be a part of it.

## CHAPTER 8

$S$he had packed way too much and it was all Sara's fault. She stood back and watched Sean load her bags on the cart, and she clutched her carry-on bag and purse. She was thankful when he didn't say anything about her heavy luggage, but just smiled at her and nodded towards the door.

"Ready?" he asked.

She nodded and then turned to her sister and brother-in-law. After hugging them both again, she straightened her shoulders and followed Sean into the airport.

"Don't be nervous," he said and winked at her.

"I'm not. I'm excited." He continued to look at her. "Okay, a little nervous." She smiled.

"I'm right there with you." They moved into line together. "Even after all the trips I've taken, I still get a little anxious when I fly."

She smiled and tried to focus on the people around her. She loved to people-watch. She did a lot of it when she went shopping at the mall in Portland, but this was differ-

87

ent. Here at the airport, there were people from all over the world.

She got so involved watching the people around her that the time in line flew by. Before she knew it, they were heading towards security.

"You thought standing in the baggage line was fun..." Sean said dryly and then chuckled as he nodded to the line at security. She sighed. It was going to be a very long day.

By the time they finally boarded and got settled on the plane, she was almost completely drained. She was also starving. She'd grabbed a bag of chips and a water from a vending machine, but they had done little to fill her stomach.

"We'll have lunch in the air," Sean said, sitting next to her.

She nodded. "I'm starved, but don't know if I can eat." She hugged her stomach and felt her nerves return.

He reached over and took her hand and smiled at her. "You'll see. You build it up in your mind and, when it's over, you'll laugh at yourself for making such a fuss over nothing."

She smiled at him. "I suppose."

By the time the instructions came over the speaker, she was gripping Sean's hand in a death grip. She was breathing quickly, and she felt a little light-headed.

Sean lifted her chin and forced her face towards his. She focused on his brown eyes and his mouth. She could barely hear what he was saying over the buzzing in her mind, but she felt his fingers on her face as he leaned closer. Her breath caught as he rested his forehead on hers, and she closed her eyes on a sigh.

"That's it, just breathe. Slowly now," he whispered and

then placed a kiss on her forehead. "Feel better?"

She opened her eyes and nodded. When he smiled, she sighed and felt her body relax a little.

"That wasn't so bad after all. Was it?"

She laughed. "Right." Shaking her head, she looked around, worried that she'd made a terrible scene.

"No one noticed," he said softly and smiled.

She glanced around and realized he was telling the truth. Everyone else around them was preoccupied with themselves.

She felt a slight shift in the plane and gripped the armrests.

"It's okay, we're just turning a little." He chuckled. "Relax."

She nodded. "Are…are we in the air yet?"

He nodded, and she could tell he was trying to not laugh at her.

She stole a glance out the small window and then closed her eyes. Not only were they in the air, but they were very far up, and the ground looked too far away.

"Relax, the worst part is over." He took her hand, gently prying her fingers from the armrests. "It's easy from here on out."

She nodded and focused on his voice. The next time she opened her eyes, Sean was handing her a cup of clear liquid. "Club soda. It might help to settle your stomach."

She nodded and took a few sips.

"Do you want some crackers?" He held up a package.

She felt settled enough after nibbling on the crackers to keep her eyes open for a while.

"I don't know how people do this, every day," she said in a low voice.

He leaned closer to her. "I just turn everything off. There was this guy we trained with, and no matter what, the second the plane engines started, he fell asleep." He shook his head and chuckled. "He didn't wake up until after the landing. Every single time he stepped in a plane he did that." He shook his head and smiled at her. "He slept for twelve hours straight one time."

"I don't think I'd want to lose control like that. No, I may not like it, but I want to see and know everything that's going on."

He smiled at her. "Here comes the food. Do you think you can eat?"

She nodded and sighed. Her shoulders had relaxcd a little. She focused on the feeling of his hand in hers and the sound of his voice until their trays were delivered.

By the time they started their descent for their first stop in Denver, she was completely relaxed. Of course, the second it was mentioned over the speakers that they were getting ready to descend, she tensed up again, but Sean was right there to help her get through it.

They had less than an hour to wait until their next flight and this time she controlled her fears more easily. By the time they finally landed in Miami, she felt like she could handle anything that came her way, as long as Sean was there to hold her hand and talk her through it.

Sean was a wreck and it had nothing to do with flying. He'd never seen someone so panicked as Becca had been when they had first taken off. He'd done his best to talk her through it, and it had seemed to work.

Holding her hand and talking to her had also helped with the nerves he felt about the entire trip. He didn't know how to handle spending more than a week with just the two of them in one of the most romantic settings known to man. He sighed as he set their bags down in their hotel room. Becca stood in front of him, looking at the small room.

"It's not as bad as I thought it would be," she said and turned to him with a smile. He could see a touch of those nerves there again.

"What? The entire day? Or the room?" He smiled.

"Everything. I've never stayed at a hotel before. Well, maybe once." She tilted her head and looked like she was thinking about something. "I guess not." She shook her head and laughed.

"Well, this isn't the best room for a first timer." It was a standard room. Two full-sized beds, a little table and chairs, a dresser, and a nightstand.

"I think it's great." She walked around and looked at everything.

He laughed and then pulled their bags out of the walkway that led to the bathroom.

"Is it going to be weird?" he said after she settled on the bed with the remote to the TV in her hands. She was flipping through channels like she'd never seen any of it before.

"What?" she asked and muted the set.

He shrugged his shoulders. "I guess we never really talked about the fact that we'd be sharing a room this entire trip."

She nodded and swallowed.

"Is it going to be weird?" He held his breath.

She shook her head slowly. "Only if we make it weird." She shrugged her shoulders and looked down at her hands.

He sighed. "Good, then let's not make it weird." He smiled, trying to hide the fact that his eyes kept roaming over her. "How about ordering room service?"

Her eyes perked up and she bounced a few times up and down. "Sounds great." She rushed over to the menu by the telephone.

They sat on separate beds, watching an old movie and eating dinner, and it killed him even more. Just the thought of her lying in the bed next to him was going to keep him up all night. He could just imagine her hair fanned out on the pillows, her dark eyelashes resting on her perfect skin. He tried to hide a sigh as he imagined how she would look.

"What time are we supposed to be at the boat?"

He chuckled. "It's a ship, not a boat."

She frowned a little but nodded.

"Four tomorrow night, but we'll need to be there early, at least two hours, to check in and go through security." She groaned, and he laughed. "At least we should have a little time to look around Miami in the morning."

Could he tell that she was nervous? She kept sneaking peeks at him, but so far, he seemed too interested in his dinner and the movie to notice. She was comfortable enough on her very own bed, across the room from him, but her insides were bubbling with nerves.

It wasn't as if they were going to sleep together, she kept telling herself. Just in the same room.

He'd asked her if it was going to be weird and she'd answered truthfully. She didn't want to be the one to make it weird, so she'd done everything she could to act like she was enjoying the time.

She'd never been anywhere and was very excited about spending some time walking around Miami tomorrow.

The short shuttle rides from the airport to the hotel hadn't given her much insight into the city, other than it was hot and sticky. She'd been too glued to the window, watching the lights go by, to care.

There were more skyscrapers than Portland, and palm trees lined the streets. She'd smiled and pointed them out to Sean, who had just nodded and smiled back at her. She knew she'd probably acted like a child the entire day, but she wasn't going to let it bother her. Plus, Sean was being such a great sport about it all that she didn't feel too bad.

But now, as the movie came to an end, she thought about having to change out of her clothes and crawl into her bed with him nearby.

Deciding to be casual about it, she jumped up. "I'm going to shower," she announced. She tossed him the remote then grabbed her small bag.

He snatched up the remote and started flipping through channels, paying no more attention to her. When she shut the bathroom door, she sighed and leaned against it.

The entire time that she showered, her mind was focused on the fact that there was a man in the next room.

She had plenty of experience with Nick, but none of it had ever involved sleeping together. They'd been kids. Once, Nick had planned on spending the night at her place when her mother had been gone, but Sara had shown up and Nick had had to go home. She'd been so excited about the possibility of sleeping in a bed with Nick that she had been in a bad mood around Sara for weeks after.

In all the time that she had been with Nick, she'd never once been nervous like this, except that first night they had been together on her birthday.

She sighed and felt like crying when she realized even some of those memories were now gone.

Pulling on her cotton pajama shorts and a tank top, she brushed through her hair slowly. She took her time brushing her teeth and applying lotion to her legs.

When she felt like she couldn't stall anymore, she packed up her bag and took one last look at herself in the mirror.

When she walked into the room, she was shocked to see Sean fast asleep on the bed, his arms tucked behind his head and his ankles crossed in a relaxed position. There was a game playing on the muted television.

She picked up the remote and switched off the set. He looked so handsome, and she wondered why she'd never really noticed it before. His dark hair had grown out a little since he'd been home, and she liked the slight curl it had.

He had a sexy, perfect chin. There wasn't a little dimple in it like Nick had, but Sean did have slight dimples when he smiled. His nose was a little crooked. Becca remembered how it got its bend and smiled. She hadn't meant to toss the football so hard; actually, she hadn't known that she could. She watched his chest rise and fall with each breath and sighed at the muscles she knew were hidden under his shirt.

Turning away, she crawled into her own bed and tried to wind down, knowing that she wasn't going to get any real sleep that night.

## CHAPTER 9

*J*ust before four that evening, they stood on the dock and looked up at the ship. They'd walked to a little coffee shop that morning for breakfast and then had enjoyed the little shops around their hotel. They'd even walked down to the water and enjoyed a nice sandwich in a bistro along the walkway. Sean had been surprised that Becca hadn't bought anything from the little stores, but she'd told him that she was saving her money for later. She did get a postcard, and she mailed it to her sister.

Now, as he looked up at the ship, he realized just how massive it was. He glanced over to see how Becca was handling it all. To his surprise, she had a huge smile on her face and looked very excited.

"Think you can handle this?" he asked, shuffling his bag under his arm.

She smiled up at him. "No sweat."

It took them a little under an hour to find their cabin and drop their bags off just inside the door.

"What do you say we go watch the send-off?" he suggested.

"Wonderful. Will there be streamers like in the movies?"

He chuckled. "Probably not, but we can hope."

She smiled, and he took her hand in his and led them back up to the deck. They probably had a small balcony in their room, but for something like this, he wanted people. Lots of people.

By the time they found a spot on the large deck, the ship was already pulling away from the docks. They stood and waved with the rest of the crowd until they were far enough that everyone started looking like little dots.

As people around them started leaving, she held onto the railing next to him with a huge smile on her face. The wind was blowing her hair as her eyes took in all the other boats in the channel. The ship maneuvered them slowly towards open water.

"Look at how green the water looks over there." She pointed to another body of water where there were smaller sailing boats parked along a row of massive houses. "I've never seen water so beautiful."

He smiled. "Get ready to see even more of it in just a few days. Not only see it but swim in it."

She smiled up at him as she pushed her hair away from her face. "I never imagined it would be this fun." She laughed as the ship finally pulled into the open water. "Oh look!" She took his hand and pulled him to the other side of the railing. "There's a swimming pool with a slide." She giggled.

He smiled. "There's a lot to explore. What do you say to take a walk before we jump into our suits?"

She nodded and tugged on his hand. He followed her as she led him around the deck, chatting about everything she saw.

By the time they'd seen everything, including the rock-climbing wall and the gym, she had listed off everything she'd like to do.

"How are we going to fit all that in?" He chuckled. "You do know that we're only on this boat for three nights?"

"Ship." She smiled as she turned around and walked backward in front of him.

"What?" He took hold of her shoulders to stop her from walking into another couple.

"It's a ship." Her smile grew.

He smiled back and nodded. "I stand corrected."

She laughed. "I think there's enough time for a dip in the pool before dinner. We walked by that steakhouse in the promenade that smelled simply wonderful."

He nodded and remembered he'd made a mental note of the place as well. "Okay, back to our cabin and then some pool time. Then we'll head back, get dressed, and hit the nightlife. Did you see the casino?"

"Boy, did I." She sighed. "I've always wanted to try my hand at gambling."

He took her hand and started walking back to their cabin.

"I tried it once when I was stuck at the Vegas airport." He shook his head. "I guess I'm not that lucky. Lost my lunch money."

She giggled. "Seriously?"

"Yeah, Nick had to buy me a sandwich."

She laughed as he opened their cabin door.

"Wow!" She said walking in. "I guess I didn't actually look at this place when we dropped the bags off." She took a few steps in and did a circle. "Oh my god!" She gasped looking up. "There's a second floor." She rushed farther into the large room.

Becca was speechless. She'd never seen anything like it. She was standing in a massive living room, and there was a small dining table and kitchenette area off to the right. There was a beautiful glass staircase that led up to the second story balcony, where she could see the edge of a bed and a sitting area.

She rushed up the stairs and walked through the sitting area into the room. Large white curtains hung on the glass wall of the balcony, so they could be shut for privacy. The bed was huge. The white comforter looked soft and inviting and the blue accent pillows, well, she wanted to shove them in her baggage for her own bed.

She turned when she heard Sean behind her. "Nice." He nodded and looked around.

"Nice?" She gawked at him. "Nice doesn't even come close."

He smiled and walked past her. "This must be the bath..." He dropped off and his chin dropped.

"What?" She rushed past him only to have her chin drop as well.

The bathroom was something straight out of the movies. Large windows were everywhere. There was a huge white bathtub with jets to the right. Lots of jets. The two gleaming white bowl sinks sat in the middle with individual mirrors hanging above them. Off to the left stood the shower. Sean walked over and chuckled. "This should make showering very interesting."

She nodded, not able to say anything. When you showered in this shower, you showered in full view of the ocean. No curtains, no fogged glass, nothing stood between you and the whole nautical world.

"It gives new meaning to being one with nature." He chuckled. "Ladies first." He nodded towards the glass enclosure.

She shook her head. "I…I think I'll stick with the bath." She turned away and hid the redness of her cheeks.

"I brought up your bags. You can change first, and then we'll head out to the pool. I guess we'll have to decide which one to go to."

"I know." She smiled. "There are four of them."

"Change. Then we'll decide."

By the time they left their cabin again, they had decided to hit the main pool tomorrow, so they headed to the smaller one closer to their cabin.

It was an adults-only pool and she was kind of grateful. Not that she didn't like kids; she loved them and had always planned on having a large family of her own someday. But, for tonight, she just wanted some quiet time soaking up the dying rays of the warm sun as they sailed off.

"It's beautiful," Sean said next to her. The pool was a little on the small side, but it was an infinity pool, giving the appearance that it dropped off the side of the boat straight into the ocean below. Seeing the sunset by the side of the pool would be a fantastic sight.

There were only four other couples at the pool and she

guessed that most of the other people were getting in their time on the big slide. "Looks like we picked correctly tonight." She stripped off her beach dress, her eyes on the cool water.

Sean was silent beside her, and she turned just in time to see him strip off his shirt and toss it on the lounge chair.

Her eyes traveled over his perfect back and she felt herself grow warmer just looking at him. When he turned around, their eyes met, and she saw heat in his eyes that matched her own. She was locked to him, unable to look away, unable to breathe unless he did. He started to move closer, just as a loud splash and the sound of laughter broke the spell.

"Well?" he said, moving a little closer to her with a smile. "Shall we cool off?"

She nodded and swallowed, trying to rein in her emotions.

When the cool water hit her, she sighed and sunk in its glory.

When she came back up, she watched Sean jump in with a loud splash. When he came up, there were a few cheers and laughs.

"Who says the adult pool can't be fun," he said, swimming beside her. She smiled and shook her head.

They watched the sunset from the cool water and enjoyed the deck and pool lights that came on as night settled in. When her stomach growled, she splashed water at Sean and nodded to the edge.

"It's food time." She smiled, and he nodded, swimming quickly over to her. He moved like a fish. It was amazing to watch him.

She'd grown up going to the Boys and Girls Club pool

every summer, but she'd never really learned how to swim very well. Watching him, she realized that he was a natural. And he looked even better wet than dry.

She sighed as she watched him step out of the pool. She thought she heard a few other women do the same, but when she looked around, everyone seemed to be involved in their own affairs.

As they walked back to their cabin, she knew for certain that she'd never get the image of him rising from the glowing blue water out of her mind.

"I'm just going to go rinse—" She stopped talking and frowned a little, remembering the shower situation.

He chuckled behind her. "I was thinking the same thing."

She turned and looked at him. "Do we have time for a bath?"

His smile grew. "Is that an invitation?"

She frowned and looked at him.

"Are we bathing together?" He smiled.

Her chin dropped a little.

He shook his head and laughed. "Go, we have plenty of time. I'll jump in when you're done."

She nodded and backed up towards the bathroom and then stopped and grabbed the bag that had all her clothes in it.

As the water filled, she dug through her bag and pulled out the perfect dress for the evening. She'd packed a few, but this one screamed what she wanted it to. At least for tonight.

She smiled and thought about the possibilities as she slowly dipped into the water. Bathing in front of a bunch of large windows didn't bother her as much as standing in front of them completely naked. After all, she was used to her life being on display. She didn't really mind her apartment overlooking the town; otherwise, she would have hung curtains months ago.

She kind of liked looking out at the town as people hurried by.

It was too dark outside to see the ocean, but she could just imagine taking a bath during the day and watching the sunrise or sunset from the jetted wonder.

She got out and quickly dressed and decided to finish her hair outside in the sitting area, so Sean could use the bath. She tucked herself into one of the fluffy robes and dragged her bags back out to the bedroom.

"I've put all my clothes in the dresser there." He pointed to the smaller one. "You can use the closet and that one." He nodded to the large dresser.

"Okay. I'll finish out here, so you have time to bathe."

He smiled. "Thanks." When he disappeared into the bathroom, she quickly got to work drying her hair and perfecting her makeup so that by the time he walked out of the restroom, she was just snapping on her bracelet.

He stepped out of the bathroom in a dark suit. His hair was combed back, giving him a very sexy Bond look. Any woman would swoon if she saw him walking towards her, looking at her the way he was now.

She felt her knees go a little weak and was thankful she was still leaning against the back of the sofa.

## CHAPTER 10

*H*e must have stepped through a portal to heaven. He'd never seen Becca looking so beautiful. Her hair was straight as it flowed around her face. The dress she wore was black and gold. The lights in the room caused the material to shine, along with her necklace and other jewelry she wore. She had on three-inch heels that were black with a tip of gold. Everything about her was perfect, down to the little matching purse she was holding.

When she smiled, he lost his breath.

"You clean up nicely," she said, taking a step towards him.

He nodded and then swallowed, feeling like an idiot.

"You're beautiful." It came out as a whisper. He shook his head. "I mean, you look beautiful."

She smiled a little more. "Thank you." He nodded and took a step towards her. "I'm starved." He stopped and frowned a little, nodding some more. "Maybe we can hit the casino after dinner?" He nodded again and wondered if he'd ever be able to speak normally around her again.

As they made their way through the halls, he noticed several eyes follow her and a sudden need for possession threatened his mind. He took deep breaths as they walked into the steakhouse to stop himself from turning her around and ordering food in their own cabin for the night.

She looked beautiful, and he couldn't blame anyone for looking at her. She was like a piece of art that he himself wanted to spend a lifetime studying.

They were seated at a small table along the large glass wall that overlooked the dark waters. A woman played soft music on a large black grand piano near the center stage.

The waiter went through the menu items and showed them their drink options and told them he'd return to take their orders shortly.

"Do you think there will be a show tonight?" Becca asked, leaning closer to him.

"I hope so. The main stage is in the family dining area, but I would think that every area would have its own show." He smiled, and she looked down at her menu.

"I can't believe all of this is paid for with the tickets."

"Everything but the drinks. I'll get us those." He smiled.

She nodded and looked down at her menu, then chuckled.

"Something funny?" He glanced over his menu at her.

"I was just thinking that if I ate like I wanted, I'd probably gain ten pounds on this trip."

He smiled. "We can hit the gym tomorrow."

"I'm sure we'll both need it. Did you see those

desserts?" She nodded towards the couple a few tables away from them.

He looked and felt his mouth water for the second time that night. "Okay, definitely hitting the gym tomorrow."

He ordered a bottle of wine, and they both ordered steak. By the time their food was delivered, a comedian had been introduced and had stepped out on the stage. They ate a wonderful dinner and laughed harder than he could remember laughing before.

Becca seemed to enjoy herself as well. When they finally left, heading towards the casino area, she wrapped her arm through his and leaned on him a little.

"I think you enjoyed that wine a little too much." He pulled her to a stop along the railing.

"Hmm, I'm enjoying everything so much." She smiled up at him and then bit her bottom lip and leaned closer to him.

He brushed back a strand of hair that had blown towards her eyes.

"You're even more beautiful in the moonlight," he whispered. Maybe he'd had a little too much to drink, as well.

She smiled. "Sean?" Her arms wrapped around his hips.

"Hmm?" he said, running his hands over the softness of her dress, of her.

"Kiss me. Kiss me in the moonlight on the bridge of—"

He dipped his head quickly and took her lips before she changed her mind.

She tasted like heaven. Her lips were soft and moved

slowly under his own. Her hands went to his hair, pulling him closer to her as his mouth took the kiss deeper.

He would have totally lost himself in her if he hadn't heard a young family approaching. It took all his willpower to gently pull away and hold onto her until they passed them.

"I can't think straight." He dipped his head and rested his forehead against hers.

"Good. That makes two of us." She pulled back and looked up at him. "Sean?"

"Yeah?" He smiled a little.

"I don't want to go to the casino anymore."

"No?" His smile fell away a little and he felt his heart skip a beat.

"No, I'd like you to take me back to the cabin and make love to me." She stood on her toes and kissed him one more time as she pushed her body up against his.

He would have given her anything at that moment. Especially when she took his hand and started walking quickly towards their cabin.

By the time his mind had cleared, they were in the corridor outside their room.

"Becca?" He watched her fumble with opening the door. She giggled a little and held a palm flat on the door as she rocked a little. Okay, so that was proof that she was a little more than just tipsy. This wasn't a good idea. He didn't want their first night to be something that she wouldn't remember, or worse, something that she regretted.

"There!" She turned as she opened the door. "I got it." Her smile was big as she grabbed his tie and pulled him into the room. When the door shut behind him, she pushed him up against it and plastered herself against him again.

"Oh, my!" He said right before her lips closed over his in a kiss that had all of his blood heading south.

Now! She wanted him now. Her lips and body vibrated against him. Couldn't he feel the power? Why weren't his hands racing over her like hers were on him? Then she realized that her hands were glued to his hair and almost giggled. Her body hadn't caught up with her mind yet.

Releasing his hair from her grip, she ran her hands over his dinner jacket and pushed it off his shoulders. When it hit the ground, she started working on his tie, only to have him grab her hands and pull back.

"Becca?" He shook his head.

"No," she said, putting a finger over his lips. "No questions. Not for tonight. Please. Let's just enjoy ourselves." She reached up slowly and pulled his tie from around his neck. "No questions tonight." She smiled and tossed the tie behind her and then reached slowly for his shirt with her eyes still on his and slowly undid each and every button.

The wine was wearing off quickly, and she hoped she'd have enough nerve to continue.

When his shirt was open for her, she pushed her hands slowly over his chest and then moved them up over his shoulders and slid them down his arms, enjoying the play of muscles beneath her fingertips.

She licked her lips and watched his eyes heat as he watched the movement. "I love the feel of you."

"My god!" It came out as a soft growl.

She smiled. "Do I make you hard?" she asked next to his skin, her breath dancing over the tiny hairs on his chest.

She felt him nod just before her tongue darted out to play over his pecs. His hands went to her hair, fisting there as she enjoyed herself, taking her time, exploring every inch, every bulge of muscle.

Then, when she dipped to go lower, to follow the dark trail of hair that led her towards her goal, he pulled on her until she stood back up.

"My turn." He smiled and backed her up until her shoulders pressed against the door. She nodded, feeling her mouth go dry.

His hands pushed hers up over her head as his mouth came back down to hers. He scooped both of her hands into one of his, circling her tiny wrists easily with one hand. His other hand traveled down her inner arm, causing little bumps to rise over her heated skin. Then he moved to her shoulder and towards her back. She heard and felt her dress zipper slowly lowering as his mouth ran down her neck, heating her skin further.

Her breath hitched as she felt her dress slide down her naked body.

"My God!" he whispered against her skin.

"You keep saying that." She smiled.

He pulled back a little and looked at her. His hands dropped to his sides as his head slowly shook. "Had I known you weren't wearing anything underneath that dress, we wouldn't have made it to dinner."

She smiled as his eyes roamed slowly over her every curve. She reached for him and pulled him back towards her.

When their skin touched, his eyes closed, and he moaned softly before he kissed her again. His hands tentatively touched her exposed skin, and then when she moved with his exploration, he started to move them faster, exploring every inch of her.

She was on fire. When she reached for the snap of his pants, his fingers settled over her wrists again. Then he quickly picked her up and started walking towards the stairs as she smiled and trailed kisses over his shoulder.

"I've never been carried before." She smiled against his skin.

"Sure, you have." He chuckled. "I carried you up your stairs just a few days ago."

She nodded. "I stand corrected. I've never been carried to bed before."

He smiled down at her as they reached the top of the stairs. "This is the week for firsts."

She nodded, feeling her mouth go dry as he smiled down at her. His dimples were showing, and his hair was messed up from her hands. The tousled look and the fact that he wasn't wearing a shirt made him look like a sexy underwear model from one of her sister's favorite magazines.

He gently laid her down on the bed and quickly disposed of his pants. The black boxer briefs clung to his thick thighs and made her mouth water.

"Are you sure?" he asked, looking down at her.

She smiled. "Sean, if you don't come down here..." She licked her lips and watched his eyes follow the movement.

He nodded and then reached into the nightstand and

pulled out a condom. She was thankful he'd thought ahead.

Then he was hovering over her. "You still have these on." She smiled and pulled on the band of his shorts.

"Slowly." He smiled. "I like savoring you." He dipped his head and ran his mouth down the curve of her neck. She arched upwards and enjoyed his hands roaming over her again. When she felt him settle between her thighs, she sighed and wrapped her legs around his hips.

"I'm trying to control myself," he said against her skin.

"I'm not." She giggled.

She could feel him smile against her. "You're asking for it."

She felt his breath on her just before he dipped down and placed a kiss on her most private spot. Her shoulders arched off the mattress as her hands dug into his hair. She thought she heard a moan escape, but she was too busy enjoying what he was doing to her to pay any attention to who had made the sound. His fingers brushed her slick skin as he lapped at her.

She'd never experienced anything like it. Nick had never. Would have never. She tossed her head from side to side, not wanting to spoil the moment by feeling guilty about Nick. No, this was her time. She only wanted to focus on her enjoyment. Hers and Sean's.

She focused on what he was doing to her, how his dark hair looked between her thighs as he pleasured her. She closed her eyes and threw back her head as she felt herself slide to a glorious finish.

She heard him moving around and when her eyes opened again, he hovered above her with a smile on his lips. "Now that's what I wanted to see," he said as he slid slowly into her.

Her eyes closed again on a moan and she felt herself building again a lot quicker than before. She knew it would be much faster than a simple slide.

Sean tried to hold out for her. He'd waited too damn long. He should have taken her downstairs, hard and fast against the door like she had wanted.

Now her hazel eyes had gone smoky and her lips were a dark pink where she'd bit them as he'd pleasured her. The tangy taste of her was still on his tongue and when he closed his eyes, he could still feel her exploding around his mouth.

Her nails dug into his hips as she pushed him to pound into her faster, harder. His arms shook as he held himself above her. Not from the exertion, but from the desire that was pulsing through his veins.

When she wrapped her legs around his hips, he jolted, causing her to squeal with delight.

"You like that?" He smiled and did it again.

She nodded as he looked down at her. She was biting her bottom lip again. He thrust deeper, harder, and watched her throw back her head with pleasure.

"Perfect," he moaned, enjoying the movement himself. Her fingernails dug farther into his skin. He would have marks there tomorrow, but he didn't care.

What mattered most to him was that watching Becca during an orgasm was almost as good as catching her in his mouth.

## CHAPTER 11

*B*ecca couldn't move, and she didn't care. For most of the night, Sean had pinned her down to the mattress. She'd stayed warm and had enjoyed the feel of his skin on hers.

At some point in the middle of the night, he'd rolled to her side and had spooned her. His arms had wrapped around her tightly, holding her next to him.

"Morning," he said into her hair. She could feel his body tense as he became fully awake.

She smiled and tried not to laugh. Turning to him, her smile fell away as she looked at him. He was perfection and for just a split second, she wondered what she'd done to deserve so much.

"I...I...ugh." He shook his head. She could tell he was fighting with something in his mind.

"I have to use the restroom," she blurted out, trying to spare them both from saying anything embarrassing.

He nodded then sighed and removed his arms from around her. When she glanced at him as she wrapped the robe around herself, he looked a little relieved, so she hurried towards the bathroom.

"Since it's still really early, I thought we'd hit the gym this morning before we tackled anything else on your list."

She stopped and thought about it. Since she'd started working at the bakery, she'd gotten used to waking early and, since most of her energy was used up in the morning, she saw no problem with spending some time at the gym. Nodding, she turned and grabbed her bag. "I'll be out quickly." He nodded.

When she closed the door behind her, she rested against it and desperately wished for a shower. Instead, she settled for a very shallow bath with no jets.

She'd packed her yoga shorts and a workout top, just in case, and was very thankful she had. She'd had a little issue packing her tennis shoes, so instead had packed a pair of walking shoes, figuring that they would do in a pinch if she needed.

As she stepped out into the bedroom, she watched Sean pull on a T-shirt and sighed. She didn't regret last night at all. In fact, she was hoping for a repeat performance soon.

He turned to her and smiled. "Shall we?"

She nodded and swallowed her lust.

When they walked into the gym, there were several other men there, but no women. She almost laughed, but then she saw the look Sean was giving a guy who was blatantly staring at her breasts.

Sean stepped in front of her and took her arm lightly. "Maybe we should…"

She whispered. "Really, you can't stop every man from staring at them." She rubbed her fingers over his arms and smiled. "I do have wonderful breasts." She giggled as she turned and started to head towards the treadmills.

By the time she had figured out how to start the machine, Sean was next to her on his own machine.

They started off at a slow walk, but when he bumped it up to a light jog, she was right there with him. Then he took it to a faster pace and she felt her competitiveness kick in. She knew she couldn't match his pace stride for stride; his legs were just too long. But she could at least make it interesting. She spiked hers up and increased the incline.

Sweat dripped down her back and neck. She'd tied her hair up on top of her head in a ponytail, which swung with each stride. She wished she'd thought to grab a bottled water from the fridge across the room, but she was enjoying herself.

Finally, when the machine beeped that it was time to start cooling down, she slowed the pace and lowered the incline. Sean slowed his machine as well.

"Doing okay?" He glanced over at her.

She nodded. She was more winded than she'd realized, so she took a couple of soothing breaths as she walked and tried to lower her heart rate.

"That was refreshing." She smiled when the machine stopped.

He chuckled. "How about some weights?" He nodded to the now cleared weight area.

"Sure." She inwardly sighed, dreaming of a cool shower and a day by the pool.

"Don't worry, I promise not to break you." He took her waist and pulled her towards the fridge. "First off, hydration." He took out two bottles and handed her one.

She drank from the bottle like she'd gone without for days. The cool liquid felt like heaven as it cooled her from the inside.

"Better?" he asked. He watched her every movement, and he'd yet to take a sip of his own water.

She nodded and then watched as he took a drink. Sweat dripped down his neck and his throat as he leaned his head back and took a large drink. She watched his Adam's apple move up and down as he swallowed. All of a sudden, she was desperately thirsty again. This time, she knew water wouldn't quench her thirst.

"Let's start off with something easy." He picked up some small dumbbells. They were covered in blue plastic and looked like children's toys. "Here, try these."

She frowned and put her hands on her hips. "Really? I get the kids toys?"

He chuckled. "Just try them." He held them out.

She walked over with a slight frown on her lips and took them. They were heavier than she'd thought. "What should I do with them?"

He smiled. "Wait, let me get some weights, then you can follow what I do." He walked over and picked up two very large black weights and then stood a few feet to her side.

He lifted his arms straight out to his sides and she followed along. After the first five, she felt her shoulders start to sting; by eight, her whole arms screamed at her. But she wasn't going to give him the satisfaction of knowing she was a complete and utter wuss. She bit her bottom lip and tried to keep up with him. In the end, she did fourteen to his twenty.

When he stopped, she was thankful. Then he started

moving his arms in a different pattern, this time bending them towards him. She tried to follow along. Tried. She probably got six done before he set his weights down and walked behind her.

"Here, hold your elbow closer." He took her right arm in his and showed her how to move. After helping her with one, he dropped his hands. "Now you try." He stayed close behind her as she lifted her right arm. "Keep your elbow in," he said next to her ear, causing little bumps to race down her neck.

Her eyes were glued to the mirror in front of them as she lifted her arm as he'd instructed. But instead of watching herself, she was focused on his dark head as he watched her.

"Good, now try the other arm," he said, moving over to her other side. His head came up and his eyes locked with hers in the mirror.

She started to lift her arm and saw his eyes heat as he watched her reflection. "Elbow in." His voice sounded a little too soft like he wasn't really paying attention.

She tucked her arm in and continued to lift. His hands came up and went to her hips, pulling her back just a little until she came up against him. She felt him grow against her back and closed her eyes on a soft moan.

"I think we're done here," he whispered, then took the weights from her and returned them to the stand.

Then he took her hand and started walking quickly out of the gym.

It was still early enough that there were only a few other people walking around. The sun was almost coming up by the time they made it back to their door. By then her heart was racing, and she was having a hard time catching her breath for reasons other than exercise.

When the door shut behind them, he pushed her up against the door. "We seem to end up here a lot," he said just before his mouth took hers in a kiss that had every muscle in her body aching.

He wasn't going to do this. Or so he had kept telling himself over and over again in the last hour. He'd wanted her again the moment he'd woken up. Before, actually. He'd dreamed about her smell, her taste, the way she'd felt in his arms.

Waking up holding her tight against his body had been heaven. Until he'd seen the look in her eyes. Instantly he'd seen that she'd regretted last night, and it had killed him.

Then it had been pure hell to watch her in the mirror at the gym. Her tight workout clothes clung to every inch of her curves. Her breasts were pushed up, and he wanted nothing more than to stare at them all day.

When he'd seen the heat in her eyes, he'd completely lost the last hold he'd had on his control. He'd grown so hard right there in the gym that he could have taken her anywhere, even there.

It had taken all his willpower to get them quickly back to their room. When he heard the door behind him click, he realized he had no plans to go another step.

He pushed her, maybe a little too fast, up against the door and kissed her as his hands yanked and pulled the tight clothes off that sexy body.

Then he pushed his fingers deep into her heat before

she had a chance to object. He was rewarded with a moan as her hips jumped towards him.

She nipped at his lips as he clamped her hands in his, holding her steady for his exploration. She was gloriously naked, and he still had his sweaty shirt and shorts on, but he didn't want to stop his torture of her, not yet. His mouth traveled over her skin, tasting her salty silkiness as he moved over her breasts. He stopped there and enjoyed how her nipples puckered on the tip of his tongue.

Soft, sexy sounds were coming from her and he wanted —no, needed—to hear more. Moving farther down, he kept moving his fingers deep into her as her hips pumped along with his rhythm. When he trailed kisses over her tight stomach, she held her breath and grabbed at his hair.

"Sean!" she gasped and tried to pull him up. "I need…"

"What?" he demanded, his voice sounding a little rough. "Tell me."

"You." Her eyes locked with his. "I need you. Now. Fast."

He nodded and felt like he'd won the best prize ever. Standing, he yanked his shorts down and put on a rubber, then pushed her legs wide and was deep in her in one quick motion.

The scream of delight that escaped her lips was his reward. His mouth captured the rest of her soft sounds as he pounded relentlessly into her. He felt her convulse around him, and he followed her quickly.

His head was resting against the back of the door as he listened to their breathing slow down. When she sighed, he smiled.

"I think we need a shower," he said as he picked her up

in one quick motion. Her eyes were closed as she nodded and wrapped her arms around his shoulders.

Not until the cool water hit them did she open her eyes again.

"What?" She tensed and looked around. They were standing in the shower, both butt naked for the entire world to see.

He chuckled. "Problem?" She moved to cover herself with her hands. He decided to distract her from her discomfort and his hands moved out, slowly running over her slick skin.

Her eyes slowly closed and a little of the tension left her body. Using some of the shampoo, he slicked her skin and rubbed some bubbles into her hair. When he moved her so that her hands braced against the glass wall in front of him, she didn't object, so he ran his hands over every inch of her back. He enjoyed watching her head roll as she moaned. She held her breath every time his fingers would brush against a sensitive area.

"You're so beautiful," he whispered against her skin. "So powerful, here." He ran a finger over her ribs. "And here." He brushed a finger lower and dipped into her again. She spread her legs a little more, giving him full access to her. The warm water was a steady stream between his shoulder blades.

When he slid into her, this time it was much slower. "Look," he said when he finally was fully embedded in her. "The sun is coming up." He smiled at the view in front of them.

She gasped a little and he felt her tense. He knew she was thinking about how they were fully exposed and was starting to focus on where they were standing.

"No, don't." He moved, stroking her from the inside and he couldn't stop his smile when she sighed and arched for him.

"It's all so…" She shook her head.

"Beautiful," he finished for her and watched her nod her head.

When their movement quickened, her fingers curled as her breath hitched. By the time they both came to completion, the sun was almost blinding them.

## CHAPTER 12

"I'm going to kill you, you know," she said as her head rested against the clear glass. He was going to die, and she was going to die from embarrassment. As soon as she could feel anything on her body again.

He chuckled and turned them until they were both under the full spray of the shower. "Reflective glass."

"What?" She pushed her hair out of her eyes.

He smiled down at her. "It's like a one-way mirror. We can see out, but no one can see in. I read all about it on the little card over there." He nodded to the counter. "We get to enjoy the full view of the ocean without anyone enjoying the full view of our moons." He chuckled.

She frowned. "How long have you known about this?"

He chuckled. "Since yesterday."

She reached up and punched him on the arm. He smiled and rubbed the spot, then nodded. "You really need to hit the gym a few more times."

She smiled. "I'm just saving up my energy." Then she

sighed and rinsed the bubbles from her hair. "I feel like climbing a mountain today, fake or otherwise."

He smiled. "First, some breakfast." He leaned down and kissed her lightly. "We're set to dock in Coco Cay this morning. We'll be there all day so I was thinking maybe we could hit the beach?"

Her excitement and smile grew. "Would those be white sandy beaches with crystal clear waters?"

He nodded. "Some of the best." He smiled.

After finishing up their shower, rather quickly, she rushed through pulling on a swimsuit, tying her hair up, and putting on a dash of makeup. She was ready almost before he was.

"Excited?" he asked as they left their cabin.

She nodded. "I can't wait to sink my toes into the sand." She sighed and tucked her arm through his.

They ate breakfast in one of the main eateries in the pavilion area. By the time they were done, the ship had already docked. She supposed that a lot of people would choose to spend an entire day on shore, but there was still so much of the ship she wanted to explore. She wanted to try her hand at the rock wall, and enjoy some of the shops along the pavilion before they hit the beach. Not to mention that she still planned on enjoying the casino later that night.

She glanced across the table and watched Sean finish off his second helping of eggs. Smiling, she leaned back and watched him.

"What?" he asked, looking up at her.

She shook her head. "You must have been hungry this morning."

His smile was quick. "Starved."

Her stomach fluttered as her smile wavered a little. She knew what he meant. She'd been starving for him as well, even after last night.

"So, what are we going to conquer first?" He leaned back and crossed his arms over his chest. She watched the muscles flex under his shirt. Shaking her head clear, she smiled.

"Shopping first, then rock climbing. Then, maybe we can try the pool with the slide before we hit the beach around lunchtime."

He nodded. "Smart. A lot of people will be at the beach, so the line for the slide should be shorter."

"Smart is my middle name." She giggled.

He chuckled. "No, it's not, it's…"

She put up her hands to stop him. "Don't you dare." She looked around and frowned as he chuckled. She cringed at her middle name, maybe because she knew that it was her father who had given it to her, or maybe because she just didn't like the sound of it. Either way, she'd never really enjoyed it and Nick and Sean had always known it.

"Still don't like it, huh?"

She shook her head. "I don't know what my parents were thinking when they named me." She shook her head. "They gave Sara a perfectly good middle name, but me…" She closed her eyes and sighed.

Over the next hour, they walked from shop to shop in the large pavilion that ran down the middle of the ship. The whole place was impressive, and, at times, she forgot they were on a ship instead of in a huge mall. They stopped at a little cupcake place called Sweet Eats and shared a very large cupcake.

By the time they made it outside and up to the higher

deck to try a turn on the large rock-climbing wall, she was feeling a little nervous.

"It's easier than it looks," Sean said from beside her. The guides were helping them into their harnesses and had already gone over all the rules.

"Really? Have you been before?" She frowned a little.

"Standard training, but I've climbed a few times for pleasure." He rolled his shoulders and started stretching his arms.

"Hmm," she said under her breath. She'd seen it done on television a lot, and there were currently very small children making it look easy on a different part of the wall. Taking a deep breath, she stepped up and gripped the first wall hold. It was brightly colored, reminding her of the weights that had deceived her earlier that day. Maybe these were going to be harder as well? She'd assumed that they would be gummy feeling, since they reminded her of a bunch of Gummy Bears, but instead, they were solid. Not quite hard plastic, but…

"Are you going to analyze it all day, or use it?" He was already a foot off the ground as he smiled down at her.

She reached higher and took hold of the highest grip she could and then hoisted herself up. She concentrated on each move she made. It was like a puzzle or a maze. Which route should she take? Which one would be easier or more challenging?

By the time she reached the top, she was a little winded and completely in love with the sport.

"Can we do it again?" She smiled over at Sean. She hadn't kept track of his climb and didn't know how long he'd been at the top waiting for her.

"Anytime you want. Have you looked at the view?" He nodded down.

Her heart skipped a few times when she looked down, but then she noticed what was around them. The ship was parked along a single long cement dock that was literally feet away from the white sandy beaches, which were filled with people. She could see people parasailing and instantly knew what she wanted to do next.

"Can we try that?" She nodded to the boat and riders.

He smiled. "It was on my list to try today."

"You've never been?" she asked, glancing at him.

He shook his head. "Not yet. How about we head out?"

She nodded and then watched him kick off from the wall. He held onto the rope while they lowered him down.

She felt her heart skip as she let go of the grips and felt herself flying outward. By the time she hit the bottom, she desperately wanted to do it all over again.

Sean felt his heart kick as they loaded them into the harness. Climbing rock walls was one thing but trusting someone with a parachute was another. His eyes ran over every cable, every connection.

"Relax," Becca said beside him, and then she reached out her hand and took his. "This is going to be fun."

"Oh, I have no doubt about that, but…" he looked over at their guides and frowned a little. The two men, including the boat captain, were all around their age. The three guys had a hard time keeping their eyes off of Becca, especially since she'd decided to just wear her swimsuit during the ride. Sure, he was shirtless too, but it was different. A lot different.

"What?" She leaned towards him as the men finished connecting them into the parasail.

"They're a little young to be trusted with this kind of stuff." He nodded to the men.

She giggled. "Is that what the military told you when they trusted you to do your job?"

He frowned. "No, of course not."

"How many times to do you think they do this in a day?" she whispered. He shrugged his shoulders. "Relax. Besides, we'll be over water the entire time."

He nodded. She was right. He didn't know what had caused him to worry in the first place. Maybe it was when he saw the guy tighten Becca's harness over her breasts and his hand had spent a little too much time there.

Finally, they released the parasail and hoisted them up slowly. He relaxed and enjoyed his time with Becca, floating over the crystal-clear water as they watched the people below them on the beach.

"The ship still looks so big from here." She nodded, and he looked.

"Look, is that our shower?" He chuckled when her eyes zeroed in, trying to find the glass. Then she glared at him.

"You'll pay for that." She smiled.

"I look forward to it." He reached over and took her hand.

"I never imagined it would be so beautiful." She sighed and started kicking her feet just a little. "I should have done this years ago."

"This?" He looked around.

"Well, not this. But I should have at least gotten out of Oregon. It would have been a good first step." She sighed again.

"I like Oregon. Don't get me wrong. Traveling is nice and I'm enjoying myself more than I have in…well, ever." He smiled. "But home is better than any cruise ship or hotel you could ever imagine."

"I don't know." She smiled over at him. "At this point I have a pretty good imagination going."

He felt heat spread through his body at her low voice. Damn, was she always going to do this to him?

"I want to spend the next few hours lying in the sand, soaking up some sun or splashing in that warm water." She sighed again.

He smiled. "That sounds perfect. As long as you add a little lunch in there." He felt his stomach growl a little.

She laughed. "I don't understand how you can eat all the time and still look as good as you do."

"If we keep working out like we did this morning, I'll need to add another meal to my day."

She laughed. "Oh!" She gasped and pointed. "Look, dolphins."

He looked off and saw a pod of them swimming a few hundred feet off the shore. "I had a close encounter with a dolphin once during a dive."

"Oh?" She leaned back a little, looking like she was totally enjoying the little trip.

"I'll tell you about it later." He smiled and kicked his feet with hers. When she just kept staring at him, he chuckled. "He swam up fast and close and for just a moment, I thought it was a shark."

"You didn't hurt it did you?"

He laughed. "No, but it took a while for my heart to start beating again."

She smiled and chuckled. "I wish we could stay up here all day." She sighed as they started pulling them back down towards the boat.

"We can do this again in Nassau."

She smiled. "If we have time. I have a whole other list of things I want to try there." She glanced at him as they landed back on the boat and he got the feeling she was talking about more than adventure items on the beach.

## CHAPTER 13

*B*y the time they left the beach almost two hours later, they were both completely relaxed.

They had played in the water until they were both a little pruned, then had napped in the sun until, finally, they were both a little too warm.

"How about cleaning this sand and sunblock off first, then a quick rest before we get ready for dinner and the casino?" she asked and then yawned a little as they walked into their cabin.

"I could lay down for a while." He reached over and wrapped his arms around her. "Are you sure you want to shower?" He smiled before he kissed her.

"Pretty sure. Especially now that I've seen that there is no way possible of seeing into those windows. They look completely blacked out from above."

He nodded and started walking towards the stairs.

"But"—she stopped him as she stood on the bottom stair— "I was actually thinking about enjoying those jets in that large tub."

His hands went to her hips as he pulled her closer. "Now that's a great idea."

His fingers skimmed under her sundress and tickled her skin.

Resting her head on his shoulder, she wrapped her arms around him. "I'm so very thankful that you decided to come along." She sighed.

"Me too," he said, holding onto her.

She'd never made love or tried to in a jetted bathtub before. It wasn't difficult, just a little awkward. They ended up giggling and laughing more than anything, until finally Sean had pulled her out, dried her off, and taken her to the bed where they stayed for the next two hours.

When she woke, she could see that the sun was just setting in the sky.

"The ship left the dock," he mumbled next to her. At first, she thought she was dreaming, but then he pulled her close and kissed her neck. "It woke me too. The subtle shift in the ship. It's just past five o'clock."

She nodded and relaxed back against him. "If I wasn't hungry, I'd want to stay right where I am for the rest of the trip."

He ran his hands over her. "So, let's order in and eat up here."

She shook her head. "I'm also very desperate to try my hand at blackjack."

"Okay, but we have plenty of time." He turned her over and started kissing her until she felt her hunger pains turn into desire.

After a quick shower, she pulled out her blue dress and decided to pile her hair up in a messy bun. She was just finishing up when Sean walked in.

"Please tell me you have something on under this one."
His voice was almost a growl.

She giggled and nodded. "I'll be good tonight." She
turned to him and rested back on the countertop.

He walked over to her and wrapped his arms around
her. "Good. That doesn't mean that I have to." He dipped
his head and kissed her until her breath was knocked from
her lungs.

When he pulled back, she gave him a shaky smile as
she wrapped her arms around his shoulders. "Does that
mean you don't have anything on underneath your suit?"
He chuckled.

They chose to eat in the main dining room.

A large stage sat in the middle of the three-story room.
Since they'd taken their time getting out the door, they
were pretty late and the place was almost completely
packed.

"We can see if there is a seat up there?" He nodded to
the second-floor balcony.

"That sounds wonderful." Instantly, she perked up. She
imagined it would be like watching an opera or play just
like in the old movies.

They found a spot near the middle and sat down just as
a waiter delivered a couple menus and glasses of water.

"The show starts in five minutes." He smiled. "I'll give
you a minute to look over the menus."

"Oh." She smiled and sighed. "Look at all the
wonderful stuff on this one." Her eyes scanned the pages.
"You know; I've never had Alaskan king crab."

He looked at her in shock. "You haven't? What's
wrong with you?" He shook his head as he smiled. "Then
it's settled. We'll both try it for the first time tonight."

133

She giggled and nodded. "This calls for champagne too. I've tried a few of the cheap bottles Patty gets in the store, but…" She made a funny face.

"Then it will be nothing but the best for tonight." He smiled and set down his menu.

The waiter came back and he ordered for the both of them. Just as the waiter left, the show started.

They ate their large crab legs, dipping them in rich butter sauce, and sipped their expensive champagne as they watched a mixture of comedy, dance, and music. She'd enjoyed herself more tonight than she had last night and knew that the evening could only get better.

By the time they walked out of the dining hall, she was itching to head into the casino.

"You're about to jump out of your skin. Is it that exciting to lose money?" He chuckled as they stopped just outside the casino.

"I don't plan on losing any." She smiled. "I'm a huge fan of the Poker channel. I watch it as often as I can."

He shook his head. "It's your dime." He took her hand. "I think I'll stick to the penny slots if they have any."

She laughed as they walked into the room and then gasped with joy as she looked around.

The lights, the sounds, everything about this place was wonderful.

"Looks just like Vegas," Sean said and led her farther inside. "Where would you like to start?"

She shook her head. "Maybe over there?" She pointed towards the tables.

"You might want to start out a little slower," he suggested.

She shook her head again. "No, I want to jump in with

both feet." She tugged on his hand until he followed her to the table she wanted.

"Blackjack, huh?" He stood next to her and watched along with her as a few hands were dealt.

"Are you going to sit?" he asked after a few minutes. She nodded, feeling just a little nervous. She'd only ever played against her friends and her sister before. Never at a professional table.

But what harm could it do? She'd agreed to only spend the cash she had brought along that night. No more. If she lost, she would just look at it as if she had paid for admission into the place.

She sat down and bought in and decided that no matter what happened now, this was the second-best night of her life.

Sean watched Becca and was shocked and amazed at how smoothly she worked the table. He couldn't call it anything other than that. In less than half an hour, she had everyone around her laughing and enjoying their time as she won hand after hand.

Some people even stopped as they walked by just to watch her. By the time she finally stood up to use the powder room, she was up five hundred dollars.

"That's some woman you've got there." The man standing next to him slapped him on the shoulder. They had been chatting while they watched. His wife sat next to Becca but wasn't having any luck. "I'd make sure to keep that one." The older man smiled at him.

The man's advice kept running through his head during

the rest of the night. They traveled from table to table while she tried her hand at the different games.

When she was up close to eight hundred dollars, after a small losing streak at the roulette table, they decided to finally try the slot machines.

"I can see where this would become addictive," she said, putting in another nickel.

He smiled and then frowned when her machine started shooting out coins as his gave him another buzz, which indicated that he'd lost again. He was down almost twenty dollars at this point and decided it wasn't worth any more of his money.

"I think you have a talent for it, or maybe it's just luck."

She laughed. "Luck? I'm not sure about that. I've never really been lucky at anything else."

He turned and watched her put more coins into the machine. "Since we've been sitting here, that machine has popped out more coins than I've shoved into mine. That's lucky."

She smiled over at him. "How about I turn all these in"—she jiggled her bucket and looked down to her latest winnings— "and buy you an ice cream cone?"

He smiled. "That would cheer me up."

They walked hand in hand towards the pavilion where there was an ice cream parlor, which even at this time of night was crowded. Instead of adults, like at the casino, kids ran around screaming and having fun as their parents sat nearby watching.

"There's a movie theater across the way," Sean said, nodding to the theater. "Want to catch a show?"

She shook her head. "I can watch movies anywhere."

She took his hand as they waited in line. "Have you ever thought about having kids?" She frowned a little when a little girl fell over next to her.

"Sure, everyone has at one point in their lives. Anyone who tells you different is either lying or denying it to themselves."

"And?" She turned to him.

"When I decide to settle down, I'd like three of them, two dogs, my own chicken coop, and maybe a couple horses or cattle. You know, to make things real interesting." He smiled.

She laughed. "Nick always wanted a large family. I guess he didn't like being an only child."

"Trust me, with my little sister Dawn running around terrorizing our lives, he knew what it was like to have a sister."

She laughed. "I can remember how bad she used to be. But she was always so cute." She sighed. "I always wanted a little brother. Having an older sister was nice, but if I could have had a brother..." She sighed. "Maybe that's why I always hung around you two so much."

He smiled and then looked down at the ice cream flavors. "Is Rocky Road still your favorite?" She nodded, and her eyes lit up, looking down at all the flavors.

They walked along the deck as they ate their ice cream. The night was so warm, and the full moon lit up the entire ocean.

"I can't believe how beautiful it is at night." Becca leaned against the railing. Instead of watching the gentle waves, Sean turned and looked at her. Her hair caught the moonlight and strands of it around her face swayed with the light breeze. He couldn't remember her ever looking so perfect. "It's just so amazing."

"What?" he asked as he brushed a strand of hair behind her ear.

"All of it." She looked at him and finished the last of her cone. She licked her lips and he sighed, wishing he could taste the sweetness. "Us, being here. I mean, I never dreamed of seeing, of doing, everything we have so far."

He chuckled, and her eyes zeroed in on his.

"I didn't mean…"

He smiled. "I know what you meant," he said, pulling her closer. "We haven't even scratched the surface. Just wait until we dock tomorrow. I've got a few things on my list that we'll tackle."

She smiled. "I look forward to seeing what they are."

"You're amazing." He cupped her chin lightly. "For someone who has never even really gotten out of her hometown, to be so unafraid of trying new things…" He shook his head a little.

"Oh, I'm afraid." Her smile faltered. "I would have never had the courage to do any of it if you hadn't been here."

When she reached up and kissed him, he knew that he felt the same way about her.

He was getting spoiled, he thought, as they walked back to their cabin. He was getting used to having her by his side, sleeping next to her, waking up with her in his arms.

## CHAPTER 14

*W*hen the ship docked the next morning, they were all packed and ready to start the next leg of the trip. A short shuttle ride took them to their hotel.

"It's massive," Becca said as she leaned a little out of the shuttle. "It's beautiful." She smiled over at him and took his hand in hers.

After checking in, they were shown up to their room, which was as the brochure described it, the Lux Signature Suite. She hadn't overheard if it was going to have an ocean view or a resort view. Either way, she was excited to see it.

When they finally walked into the room, she was too occupied with the view and the large room to pay any attention as Sean helped unload their bags and tipped the bellhop. The room was gorgeous with its crisp white bed and furniture. There was a large jet tub in the bathroom that she looked forward to enjoying. Even the sitting area was perfect. It sat next to the large windows, overlooking a green oasis that sat between them and the white sands and teal waters.

"Like it?" he asked, coming up behind her and wrapping his arms around her waist.

She could only nod. "I've never seen anything more beautiful. Look at how green and blue everything is." She turned in his arms and hugged him back. "Thank you for coming with me."

He nodded. "What shall we do first?" He sighed into her hair and she felt little goose bumps rise all over her skin.

She ran her hands up his back and had a good idea what she wanted to do first. He must have guessed, because he chuckled and nodded, then started to walk her backward towards the bed.

"I thought you'd never ask." He laughed as they fell back onto the bed together.

A little over an hour later, they stood on the white beach in their swimsuits. They had rented snorkeling gear. She'd never been snorkeling and was a little nervous. Since there had been too many people right by their hotel's beach, they had walked down some ways until there were fewer people splashing about in the shallow waters.

"It's easy," Sean said, sitting down in the sand next to her. "I'll go over some basics. This"—he tugged lightly on her mask— "is, of course, your mask." He smiled when she gave him a look. "Okay, let's take it up a step. If your mask fills up when you're underwater, don't take it off." He put his mask on and then showed her as he explained how to gently pull it away from your face and blow air out your nose to clear it. "We'll practice it in the water before heading out too far." She nodded and looked down at her breathing tube.

"What about this?" She held it up. "I used one like this at the pool when I was a kid."

"Probably not like this. These ones have a purge valve. It allows you to pinch here"—he showed her the small clear plastic area— "while you're under to clear any water that's gotten in your tube. Short bursts of air from your mouth and it will clear out."

She nodded and thought of how scary it might be to be under with water coming into her tube.

"I got certified to dive," she said, looking over at him. "But they didn't go over snorkeling. I guess I should have taken the extra class." She smiled.

"Seriously?" He looked at her. "You're certified to dive?"

She nodded. "Two years ago, Nick and I had talked about it and we both thought it was a good idea. They have a class at the Boys and Girls Club that I took."

He smiled. "This opens up the possibilities for us in the next few days. I'll look into seeing if we can go out."

She nodded. "I'd love to. I only ever went to the pool. But to finish the class off, we went down to the beach and practiced in the surf. It was freezing that day." She shivered remembering.

He chuckled. "Let's go get wet, and then I'll show you more."

They spent almost ten minutes in the shallow water before Sean was confident in her abilities. She grabbed her underwater camera and tied it to her wrist, then followed him out to deeper water. It was amazing. They held hands as they swam and watched the sea life below them.

She had a screen saver on her computer of brightly colored underwater coral and fish. It paled in comparison to what they were seeing now.

She stopped and took several pictures and turned the camera on themselves as they floated along the surface. When Sean pointed downwards, she felt those nerves kick in as she nodded and followed him to the bottom of the ocean floor. It took her three short dives to finally become comfortable.

Around lunchtime, he pointed to the shore. "I'm starved." He smiled. "I saw a place to eat lunch by the pool." She nodded. "I thought we might rent a Jet Ski after lunch for a while."

"I'd love to." She'd gone Jet Skiing several times and had thoroughly enjoyed the power of flying through the water.

Stowing their gear back in the bags and returning them to the rental place, they walked hand in hand back up to the large pool area.

After sandwiches and bottled water, they walked down the beach to the Jet Ski rental area.

Sean loved the way Becca held on behind him. Her arms and chest were glued to him as he gunned the Jet Ski. It had been years since he'd had so much fun in the water. She laughed behind him and tugged on him to look at different things along the way.

He made her hang onto him, even more, when he started showing off a little by sending the Jet Ski in tight circles. She squealed and held on and laughed when they finally came to a stop.

"That was so much fun," she said, pushing some wet hair out of her eyes.

He laughed and glanced back at her. "Now it's your turn."

She smiled. "I thought you'd never give up the reins," she said and then frowned a little.

He could tell what she was thinking. How to get in front without going overboard.

"You can figure it out." He smiled. "Climb over me." What happened next was pure torture. She clung to him as she reversed their positions. Every inch of her almost naked wet body touched every inch of his. By the time she sat in front of him, they were both a little breathless.

His hands reached up to stop her from turning the Jet Ski back on. Then he was twisting her and taking her mouth with his until he could think only about taking her.

When she pulled away from him, she rested her head against his. "You make me forget about everything else." She smiled up at him. Her hands went to his face as she kissed him one more time quickly. "Now, sit back and be prepared to get wet." She laughed as she turned around and started the Jet Ski.

By the time he finally tapped her shoulder to signal that they needed to head back in, he was more than impressed by her driving skills.

"What should we do now?" she asked as she removed her life vest.

He couldn't stop watching how her chest rose and fell with every breath. Smiling a little, he nodded. "We could go back and take another nap." He pulled her closer and kissed her some more.

When he pulled back, she smiled and nodded. As they made their way back to their hotel room, he wondered if he'd ever stop wanting her as badly as he did now.

"I have something special lined up for us tomorrow," he said when they were alone in the elevator.

"Oh?" She wrapped her arms around him and leaned into his body. "Do I get a hint?" She teased him, and he felt himself start to shake with want.

"If you keep this up, I'll tell you everything."

She giggled and kissed him one more time before the elevator doors opened. It seemed to take forever to get back into their room. Even though they only had their swimsuits on, it felt like an eternity before they were finally skin to skin. He pulled her into the shower and made love to her under the cool spray and then carried her to the bed and enjoyed watching her face as he pleased her over and over again.

By the time his stomach growled, they were both showered and dressing for their first evening out on the island. He'd looked into which places to eat and decided to stay near the hotel for the night. There was a casino just a few buildings down and when they walked into the restaurant next door to it, he knew he'd picked the right place.

"Oh my," she said under her breath when the wonderful smells hit them.

He glanced down at her and felt his mouth water. She'd worn a little red number tonight with red wispy feathers on her shoulders. Her red heels made her taller, and he very much enjoyed the look.

"It smells like heaven in here," she whispered as they

were shown to their table, which was right next to a large window. The sun was just setting, and they watched the bright colors fill the sky. Becca took a few pictures, and when the waiter stopped by, he asked if they wanted a picture together. Sean pulled his chair closer to hers and smiled as he wrapped his arm around her.

He ordered a bottle of white wine, knowing what she liked the best, and then they looked over the menu.

"This sounds wonderful." She glanced up at him and tapped her menu. "The rock lobster."

He'd been interested in that one himself, so he nodded. "For me, it was between that and the baked bonefish. I haven't decided yet."

She smiled and leaned closer. "I'll get the lobster, you get the bonefish, and we'll share."

He nodded and reached over to take her hand. "Sounds like a plan."

"Of course, I'll want my very own dessert." She smiled over at him as he chuckled.

He'd never experienced food as good as this. Well, maybe at the Golden Oar, but the fact that they were thousands of miles away from there assured him that it was okay to indulge in the comparison.

"Do you think it's possible to gain ten pounds on vacation?" she asked when she was finished eating, leaning back in her chair and rubbing her flat stomach.

He laughed. "On me, yes. You?" He shook his head. "Do we need to hit the gym again?" He smiled when he saw her face heat.

"Maybe a brisk walk on the beach tomorrow morning. You know, to watch the sunrise."

He smiled. "How about a slow one tonight as the moon

145

rises?" He reached over and took her hand again. She nodded and smiled.

When they stepped onto the warm sand and the cool night air hit them, he knew he'd remember everything from that moment. She leaned down and removed her skimpy shoes and dangled them from her hand as he held her other hand, and they walked towards the water.

"You look simply amazing in red," he said offhand. She stopped walking and smiled over at him.

"You look pretty dashing in gray." She reached over and took his dinner jacket in her hands and pulled him closer. "Did you ever imagine?" She shook her head and sighed. "I told myself I wasn't going to do this," she said, looking off towards the dark water.

"Do what?" He pulled her closer. "Think of what it would be like to be here with Nick instead?"

Her eyes searched his and then she nodded slowly.

"It's okay. I've thought about him a million times already on this trip." He sighed and looked off towards the water himself. "He would have loved it here."

She nodded. "Although I don't know if he would have fought me over the last piece of my lobster tail tonight." She giggled.

"Oh?" He looked down at her.

She shook her head. "He was allergic to shellfish. Remember?"

He chuckled. "That's right. I'd almost forgotten."

"I've forgotten a lot." Her voice sounded a little sad.

"It's okay to forget some things. What matters most is that we have the truly great times in our memories. Those will never go away."

She nodded her head and leaned back against his chest

as they watched a boat flooded with little lights float by them in the water.

"It helps," she said and turned towards him, "that we fit together like we do." He watched her face flush in the dim lights and waited. "Personality-wise," she finished.

He nodded. "That was never a problem with us. Remember when we used to gang up on Nick." He chuckled as she smiled.

"Like prom." She giggled as he tried to remember. "We wanted to vote for The Great Gatsby theme, he wanted to vote for the Fifty's Rock theme."

He nodded, remembering the argument the three of them had about it. "We won and yet, for some reason, I still think he voted the other way."

She chuckled. "It was fun wearing that hooped skirt though. I think everyone in our class was against us."

"The entire football team wanted to wear black leather jackets and grease their hair back." He smiled and then sighed. "Well, we've got an early day tomorrow." He glanced at his watch, which he'd forgotten to set to local time.

"How early? You know I was just joking about the brisk walk at sunrise."

He laughed. "We'll need to be dressed and have eaten breakfast by eight. That's not too early for someone who has been waking up at four every day for the last couple years."

She nodded. "I can do eight." They turned and started walking back towards their hotel. There were lighted tiki lamps leading the way.

"I wish I could take the sand and water with us. Can you imagine having a beach like this in Pride?"

He smiled. "Something tells me that everyone who lives in Pride is glad that our beaches are cooler and don't fill up with a million tourists each year."

"I suppose you're right. I guess the sticky weather would get old." She sighed. "And I do enjoy a good rain in the spring and being snowed in during one of our big storms during the winter."

His mind flashed to a scene of the two of them in front of a fireplace, being snowed in together. He wanted it more than anything else he'd ever wanted in his life.

## CHAPTER 15

The next morning, she stood in the lobby in shorts, a tank top with a button-up over it, and tennis shoes. She'd worn her swimsuit underneath it all, just in case.

Sean wouldn't tell her exactly what they were doing. He had picked out her clothes and made sure she'd worn the right thing for his secret plans. They'd grabbed muffins in the eatery in the hotel lobby, and she'd downed a whole thing of orange juice, while he'd sucked down two cups of coffee.

"I don't know how you live the life you do without coffee." He shook his head and looked at her as they waited for a shuttle, which would take them to their next adventure.

"Coffee makes my heart go nuts," she said.

"I thought that was my job?" He chuckled as a tour bus arrived. There were almost a dozen other people waiting for the bus, as well.

When they entered, he pulled her into a seat and handed her a brochure.

"Okay, so it's not any one thing we're tackling today, but many." He nodded to the paper in her hand.

"It's a tour?" She smiled at him. "Of the whole island?"

He nodded. "I thought we might as well get to know a little about where we are."

"Oh, I love it." She leaned over and hugged him, then went back to scouring the brochure. "I can't wait. It's a good thing I cleared this off last night." She tapped her phone. "I've taken more pictures on this trip than I did all last year." She chuckled.

"The first stop is on Paradise Island." He reached over and took her hand. "It's just a few minutes from here."

"The Cloister," she read from the paper and then continued to read its history. "I'm a huge history buff." She glanced at him."

He chuckled. "I remember. You used to help Nick and me with all our history homework."

She nodded. "It's what I want to teach," she said a little nervously. She didn't know why, but just saying it out loud made her feel better.

He smiled and squeezed her hand. "You'll be great at it."

She chuckled. "If my sister doesn't kill me when I tell her I have to cut back my hours, so I can go to school."

He shrugged his shoulders. "Who knows, maybe I'll fill in for you."

She laughed. "Right. You, working for my sister in a bakery." She shook her head. "No, you would get fat, trying everything on the menu."

He laughed. "Okay, so maybe not."

"Don't worry about deciding on what you want to do." She could see his eyes grow a little distant. "Something will come to you when you least expect it. When it does, you'll just know that it was meant to be," she said as the bus pulled away from their hotel.

The driver spoke over the little speakers as he drove, telling everyone the history of the island and pointing out anything of interest. She listened intently and took pictures out the open windows.

She enjoyed seeing the police officers standing on their little boxes with their makeshift tops at each intersection as they directed traffic. The bus passed a little market area, which was crowded. She desperately wanted to get off the bus and go exploring. Then they turned a corner and the Cloister came into view.

They were ruins of an old building. High arches and columns circled the entire first floor. Wide stone stairs took you past a green lawn with bushes, stone benches, and statues.

The bus parked, and the driver told everyone that they had twenty minutes to explore. She grabbed Sean's hand and tugged him along, taking pictures as they went.

Flower beds full of colorful flowers she'd never seen before were everywhere. When they were done exploring inside the open walls, they moved to the back area, where more stairs led them down a path towards the water. A beautiful gazebo-type structure sat at the end of the pathway. She took over a dozen pictures of the structure from all different angles.

Tall statues lined the walkways. There was an old pond

that was lined with stone, and another tall statue stood in the middle of the water.

"It looks like some English gardens that I've seen in books." She sighed and took another picture of Sean standing next to a column.

A woman took their picture together as they sat near the pond on a bench. She knew she'd treasure that one, just as much as she would the one their waiter had taken last night as the sun set behind them in the restaurant.

"I can't believe anything else I see today will top that." She sighed as the bus started pulling away.

He chuckled. "Have you read about our next stops?"

She shook her head and looked down at the pamphlet he'd given her. She'd been too busy learning about the island's history before.

"A fort?" She felt her heart jump as excitement ran through her. "Fort Charlotte." She read out loud.

"I remember the school trip we took to Fort Stevens. You didn't let Nick, or I talk to you the entire time, just in case you missed something." He smiled, and she felt her heart skip again. Did he remember that? It was so nice having that history with someone.

When the bus stopped again, the driver let them know that they would have another twenty minutes to explore The Queen's Staircase. She glanced down and read how it was built in limestone by the slaves to honor Queen Victoria's help in abolishing slavery in the Bahamas.

They walked with the rest of the group through a narrow pathway lined with tall limestone walls that were covered by moss. Everyone made their way towards the tall staircase near the end. Off to the left, there was a small waterfall. Water ran over smooth tall stones into a clear pool near the bottom.

"It looks like something out of an Indiana Jones movie. You almost expect to look up and see the big stone rock chasing after you." She laughed at his joke.

"It does." She nodded. "We might just have to buy you a Fedora." She smiled and placed a kiss on his mouth.

They climbed the stairs, and she took pictures from the top. There was a small garden area up there, but they had spent too much time enjoying themselves below and were running out of time to explore.

"I hope they give us more time at the fort." She frowned a little.

"We'll have two hours there, and it includes enough time for lunch at a place called the Fish Fry." He smiled. "I'm told they have the best seafood on the island."

She nodded. "Perfect."

The fort was only five minutes from the staircase. They passed the brightly colored seafood place on the way to the parking lot.

"We can walk back down here." He nodded. "See, there's the fort." Her eyes were already glued to the gray stone ahead of them.

Becca felt like she'd been hiding her desires for so long. She'd denied herself the true pleasure of learning history. Glancing over at Sean as everyone else got off the bus, she knew that because of him, she wouldn't have to hide it anymore.

Sean had never seen someone so excited about walking

around a bunch of rocks before. Sure, the old iron guns were pretty cool, but he just couldn't see the draw of the rest of it. But he watched her and smiled when she'd read off some of the history from the small plaques that were around.

Finally, when he thought that she'd seen everything, he tugged on her hand until they were on the path towards the wonderful smells at the Fish Fry.

They sat out at a bright blue table and had some of the best-fried fish and shrimp he'd had in years.

He chased it all down with a cold beer while Becca had an iced tea.

"You two are staying at the Lux, aren't you?" someone said from behind him.

"Yes," Becca answered with a smile. He turned to see an older couple and their teenage son sitting at the orange table next to them.

"We saw you on the cruise too. We're staying for six nights. How long are you two here for?"

"Four," Becca said easily. "Where are you from?" she asked them.

The woman chuckled. "A small town on the border of Washington and Oregon."

"We're from Oregon ourselves," Sean said, turning a little so he could see the family. He reached out and, after introductions, they started chatting with Barbara, Stan, and their son, Ronny.

Stan was a retired principal and Barbara was still teaching high school geometry. Ronny, who had just turned seventeen, looked like he'd rather be anywhere than sitting in the Bahamas with his folks. Sean did notice that at least the kid wasn't on some sort of game or cell phone, wasting his time. Instead, he sat and listened to their conversation, answering any questions his parents asked.

It turned out that the Hammonds lived less than an hour from Pride. Though they had never visited the small town before, they had heard of it. Barbara was an avid lotto player and had always promised her family a trip to the Bahamas if she ever won. Well, last month she hit the big jackpot of two point five million.

"So, I booked the first available cruise, and here we are." She beamed.

"I've never met anyone who's won the lottery before." Becca smiled. "Of course, I've never played the lottery before, either." Everyone laughed.

"We've booked a charter boat tomorrow. They're supposed to take us out scuba diving and fishing. There's plenty of room for two more. If you aren't certified, you're welcome to fish with me. That is if you two want to tag along," Stan said as they were all walking back towards the bus.

"Actually, we were just talking yesterday about looking into going out. We're both certified." Sean looked towards Becca who gave him a big thumb up.

"Sounds like a plan," Sean said. "I can see about renting some gear when we get back." He tried to remember if the snorkeling place had scuba gear or not.

"If you can't find any, I'm sure the company we hired to take us out has more for rent," Barbara said. "Well, this was just the loveliest day I've had all year." She smiled as they walked back towards the bus.

When they sat back down on the bus in front of the family, Becca turned towards Barbara and said, "I'm wanting to finish my schooling and become a teacher."

"Oh." The woman's smile grew. "What do you want to teach?"

"History, but I don't think I'm quite ready for high school kids yet."

Barbara laughed. "I wasn't ready either until Ronny, here, turned thirteen."

"You still aren't, honey," Stan broke in and everyone laughed while Ronny sat and looked out the window.

When the bus stopped in front of their next stop, Ronny perked up a little.

"What stop is this?" Becca asked, looking down at the paper.

"Bat caves," Ronny said, smiling for the first time.

"Bats?" Becca said in a soft voice. Sean could instantly see her skin crawl.

"You don't have to go in if you don't want," Sean said next to her.

She nodded. "I think I'll listen to the guide but stay outside with the other squeamish people." He watched her shake a little.

"Look at how that kid's face lit up when they mentioned bats," Sean said to Becca.

"He's a teenage boy. Remember we took that trip to the zoo when you and Nick were his age." He remembered that trip.

"So?" He frowned a little.

She shook her head then whispered. "All you and Nick wanted to see were the monkeys doing it." She chuckled and then covered her mouth when Ronny looked over at them.

Sean smiled. "Yeah, teenage boys." He looked towards

Ronny who was busy listening to the guide talk about the bats like it was the most interesting thing in the world.

Sean sat out on the patio area with Becca while the rest of the brave group walked down towards the caves. They shared a large drink in a coconut and enjoyed the shade as colorful birds flew overhead.

The bus ride back to the hotel was full of Ronny talking. Even his parents looked surprised at how excited the kid was about the nocturnal creatures.

"We're leaving from dock three around seven tomorrow. They told us not to worry about lunch, but you'd better make sure you have some breakfast before we head out. We're not supposed to be back until two in the afternoon," Barbara said as they stood out front of the hotel.

"We'll be there." Becca hugged the woman and waved goodbye to the men.

"What a wonderful family." She sighed as she wrapped her arm around Sean as they walked back towards their elevator. "What a wonderful day."

"I'm glad you enjoyed it. I was thinking about finishing the day off with a scooter ride through town and finding someplace to have dinner."

She smiled. "Sounds wonderful. First, I'd like to change." She looked down at her shorts and shirt.

He nodded. "A shower and a change do sound wonderful."

# CHAPTER 16

She'd never driven a scooter before, but after five minutes of putting along the road, she was seriously thinking about buying one for herself.

It wasn't just fun; it was a blast. Sean drove next to her on his own scooter as they made their way from the hotel to the heart of Nassau.

They stopped at the little market she'd seen before, and he bought her a rope bracelet she admired. Sean bought a couple souvenirs for his parents while she looked for something for Sara and Allen. It was actually Sean who found the perfect gift in one of the smallest stores.

He held up a set of shirts. There was a woman's shirt that said Bahama Mama, a large one that said Bahama Dada, and then a baby's shirt that said, Bahama Baby.

"They are perfect." She held up the little shirt and felt a wave of nostalgia hit her. Her sister was going to have a baby. She shook her head and smiled. "It's hard to believe that in less than eight months, I'll be an aunt." She smiled at Sean as she paid for the shirts.

He smiled and then frowned when his stomach growled loudly. "All of this shopping has given me a huge appetite."

"I saw a place that looked good." She tucked her bags under her arm and grabbed his hand.

He followed her until they stood in front of a place called the Poop Deck. They had tables and chairs outside facing the water and when they walked up, they were seated quickly outside near the side on the patio area.

"I can see our hotel from here," he said, nodding past the row of boats tied to the docks they were overlooking.

She followed his gaze and smiled, then looked at the large bridge they had crossed on the way over. That was the only part of her journey that she hadn't liked. If they had been on a bus or a car, she wouldn't have minded, but on the scooter, it had been a little too open for her liking.

"We can find another way back." He reached out and took her hand, guessing what she was thinking by her look.

"No, it's okay. I need to learn to face my fears. Besides, after everything else we've done on this trip, driving over a bridge on a scooter is nothing."

He chuckled.

They ate fried calamari and grilled shrimp and split the largest lobster tail either of them had ever seen.

By the time they made it back to their hotel, Becca was more than a little tired.

"I can't believe how much we packed into today. It will be nice enjoying ourselves out on the water tomorrow." She sighed as she dropped her bags inside the door. The sun had gone down as they had driven back over the bridge.

When she took off her sandals, she sighed.

"Here." He walked over and took her hand in his, then led her to the bed. "Lie down." He nudged her until she lay on the bed, face down.

When he moved over her, she felt every nerve in her body start to vibrate. Then he started kneading her shoulders, and she simply melted.

"Mmm, that feels so good," she said against the comforter.

He chuckled a little as her entire body relaxed in his hands. When his fingers started pushing and moving her clothing aside, she moved and pushed right along with him, trying to get as naked as he wanted. The entire time, his fingers continued to work their magic on her sore muscles.

"You have a talent for this," she mumbled. "Maybe you should do *this* for a living." She chuckled.

"Would you really want me doing *this*…"—he leaned down and placed his mouth on the skin between her shoulders— "to another woman?"

She quickly shook her head no.

"What about *this*…" His mouth dipped lower. "Or…" His hands ran over her hips, pulling her long cotton skirt down until she was completely naked before him.

He used his hands to push her legs wider until she was fully exposed to his view. Then he stood up and yanked off his own clothing quickly.

"So beautiful," he whispered as he came back to her and ran a fingertip over the curve of her back. "So soft." His finger traveled lower until she felt it brush against her soft skin, which was slick from wanting him.

"Sean," she moaned and grabbed fistfuls of the comforter.

"Do you like that?" he asked, and she could hear the humor in his voice.

Nodding her head, she bit back a plea as he brushed his fingers over her again.

"Tell me, Becca. Tell me what you want. Anything. I'll do anything you ask."

She moaned as his hands rubbed over her skin, heating her from the inside.

"Touch me, Sean." She sighed when he did. "Push your fingers into me." Her voice hitched when he moved quickly to obey her. "Now, move." Her hips pumped, showing him what she wanted.

"Anything," he whispered next to her ear.

"Kiss me." Her body moved with his as his mouth trailed down her back, her sides. "Lower. I want your mouth on me." She sighed when he finally reached her goal.

"Open for me darling," he said against her skin. "Spread your legs wider." He nudged her knees.

She bit the comforter when his tongue rested on her lips and then dipped inside her for a taste.

One of his hands was pressed against her lower back, keeping her glued to the bed as he pleasured her, doing everything she asked.

Then, when she felt herself building quickly, he gently flipped her onto her back and continued using his mouth and hands to bring her to her breaking point.

Only when she cried out his name did he come to her. She wrapped her legs around his hips as he slid slowly into her heat. She held on as he took his own pleasure, letting her build up faster and faster until she felt herself tense, just before he growled her name in her ear.

❄

That was it for Sean. It was all over. At that exact moment, he knew he was in love with Becca. Hell, he'd probably fallen in love the second he'd seen her crying in his clubhouse outside his childhood home.

But his mind hadn't caught up with his body until just that instant. Not that his mind had been in control a moment ago, but at that second, he just knew.

Like she'd said, once you know what you want for your future, you'll just know. Well, he knew. He wanted Becca. No questions asked.

He could hear her breathing slowly next to him and knew that she was asleep. With a busy day in the water planned for tomorrow, he knew he needed his own rest, but his mind refused to shut down. Not with the new enlightenment screaming in his mind.

So many questions ran through his head. How could he get Becca to feel the same way about him? Did she already? Would she?

He ran the same questions through his head for half an hour, and then he finally drifted off as he held the woman he loved.

The next morning, they were right on time getting to the docks. They were loaded down with the scuba equipment they'd rented. Stan and Ronny helped him load it onto the boat. There were three crew members, but they were busy loading the other equipment that they would need for the day.

Becca and Barbara chatted as they pulled away from the dock, so Sean talked to the men about fishing and scuba diving. Stan told him that Ronny had been certified when he was eleven.

"We used to live in California before I retired." Stan shook his head. "Couldn't get out of the Valley fast enough. Course, Ronny here took the move the hardest." He nodded to his son who was busy checking out the chest full of fish bait. "Well, up until he met a girl earlier this year." He whispered and smiled. "Now, of course, he doesn't want to even go on vacation with his folks without being attached to his phone."

Sean smiled. "I was wondering why he wasn't glued to a phone or game yesterday."

Stan laughed. "We took it away the first night. Actually, we put all our phones away for the entire trip." He nodded to the camera around Barbara's neck. "We all agreed that we'd take the pictures on that and upload them each night. But the day and our time is for seeing the world, not a small screen, chatting with people we can talk to when we get home."

Sean nodded. "It takes guts for a kid his age to give up anything electronic."

Stan smiled. "Yeah, he's a good kid, if not a little wild every now and then." He sighed. "He's been having a hard time at the new school. His grades are suffering, and he's been reprimanded for fighting. Twice." He shook his head. "It took a lot of smooth talking to convince the school not to kick him out."

Sean looked over at the kid and thought back to the few fights he'd gotten into when he was his age.

"Teenage hormones," Sean said and patted Stan on the back. "It'll all settle down sooner or later."

"Well, we hope so." Then he smiled. "Looks like

we've reached our destination." He nodded and saw that there were already other boats with scuba divers preparing to dive in. "Let's get ready, shall we?"

They had brought extra tanks along, so they all decided the first trip would be their shortest, staying down for only twenty minutes. He glanced at his diving watch and looked over at Becca, who looked a little nervous.

"You got this?" he asked, reaching out for her hand.

She nodded. "Piece of cake." She smiled, but he could still see the worry that she tried to mask.

"I'll be right there the entire time." He smiled and squeezed her hand. "Ready?"

She nodded, and he watched her flip off the side of the boat and into the water like a pro.

He followed her and when he hit the water, instinct kicked in. Diving was like breathing to him. He knew everything there was to know about it. He loved it. He lived for it. And, for the second time in the last twenty-four hours, he knew what he wanted to do with his future. He hadn't thought that teaching would be his lot in life, but teaching something he loved, just fit.

He followed her as she moved downward, heading to a larger crop of coral that the guides had talked to them about.

Her camera was out and flashing as she spotted a school of fish. He pointed out a green eel poking its head out near the bottom, and she moved a little closer to snap a shot.

He kept his eye on his watch and when it was time, signaled for her to head towards the surface. When they broke the water, he had to admit, he was impressed with her skill.

They loaded in the boat and she started to remove her gear, smiling at him the entire time.

"Did you see the striped fish and the yellow ones?"

"Banded butterflyfish are the striped ones. The yellow ones are reef butterfly. Beautiful, weren't they?"

She nodded. "I hope my pictures come out alright."

He smiled. "They should; the flash was bright enough." He chuckled. "Did you feel okay in the water?"

She sighed and smiled. "Like a fish." She turned to him. "You looked pretty comfortable yourself." He smiled as he watched the Hammond family climb back aboard. "Yeah." He shook his head and felt a sting behind his eyes. "It's what I'm made to do." He took her hand. "I think I've decided what I want in life." He tugged on her hand and wished more than anything that they were alone.

"Have you see Ronny?" Barbara asked them as she looked around. "We gave him the signal to come up, but well, I guess we beat him back to the surface." She frowned as she glanced over the side of the boat.

"He still has air left; maybe he's just taking his time," Stan said, sitting down and removing his own tank.

"Stan, please. Could you just..." Barbara nodded towards the back of the boat.

"I'll go." Sean stood up and grabbed a fresh tank. He made his way towards the back of the boat.

"We were over by the big arch in the coral. He had spotted some crabs he wanted to look at," Barbara said, biting her bottom lip.

"Don't worry; I'm sure I'll run into him on the way up." He smiled and checked his mask and his tank before flipping back into the water.

He thought for sure he'd meet the kid on the way up,

but he made it to the bottom and started heading towards the coral area without seeing him. When he got there, he looked around and still no kid. He looked everywhere. Not until he knew the kid would be close to maxing out his oxygen did he finally spot him snapping pictures of an octopus. Just as he got to Ronny's side, the thing let out a big plume of ink in the kid's direction. He chuckled a little as the kid started whaling his arms around, trying to get the ink to clear.

Wrapping his hand around the kid's skinny arm, Sean pointed upward and then at his watch. Ronny nodded that he'd follow, but Sean made sure to keep his hand locked around the kid's arm as they started to make their way upwards.

They were almost a quarter of the way up when Ronny started tugging on him quickly. He looked over and the kid started giving him the sign that he'd run out of oxygen. Taking a breath, he handed him his regulator just as a big burst of hot water rushed between them. The kid went one way; Sean was pushed another. The only thing holding them together was his hand locked around the kid's skinny arm.

Sean's lungs screamed for a breath since it had just been knocked out of him. But he held still and was thankful when the world righted itself that Ronny had gotten the regulator into his mouth and had been sucking on air during the whole ordeal.

He smiled at the kid and gave him a thumb up sign. The kid nodded his head. They swam upward for a while, sharing the oxygen as they went. He knew they would be coming up far from the boat, but a little swim above water couldn't hurt.

They were almost halfway up to the surface when Ronny tried to hand the regulator back to him and another wave hit Sean full force in the chest. This time panic set it as they were pushed apart more quickly. He watched, almost in slow motion, as Ronny let go of the regulator. He watched in horror as the kid was pushed away from him so quickly, he didn't have time to react.

Sean swam with all his might, fighting against the strong currents as they threatened to pull them even farther apart. He knew that any distance, even the smallest could easily mean death for the kid. Using every muscle, he had in his legs, he kicked as hard and fast as he could until he was inches from the kid's ankle.

When his fingers wrapped around Ronny's skinny bones, he gripped it as tightly as he could. The kid wasn't kicking, and Sean could tell that he'd lost consciousness. Just then, Sean felt another wave of hot water pushing him again from behind. This time, however, there was nothing that could cause him to loosen his grip on the kid.

## CHAPTER 17

*B*ecca sat with Barbara and tried to calm the mother down by telling her how good Sean was at his job. She asked her questions about Ronny and where they were from, but when her husband signaled that Ronny would soon be out of oxygen, even Becca began to panic, and the women gripped each other as the captain made the calls for help.

Stan grabbed a fresh tank and, along with two of the crewmen, jumped in the water and started the search.

Minutes seemed like hours, hours seemed like years as they sat on the boat waiting. The time came and went quickly for Sean's tank to run out of oxygen.

Even though it was in the high nineties, Becca couldn't stop her body from shaking. Blankets were wrapped around her as she was asked question after question by the Coast Guard, who had arrived less than ten minutes after being called.

She, Barbara, and Stan were shuffled onto another

larger boat and taken back to shore. She had objected but hadn't been able to put them off

Somehow, night had set in without her noticing. She didn't even remember the sun moving. She was handed food and water and alongside the Hammonds, she ate.

She was walked up to her room and was asked to stay put, in case word came. She nodded to the female officer and shut the door behind her.

She collapsed against the door as complete and utter terror shook every bone in her body. She didn't know how long she lay there, but she finally got up when the ringing of her phone jolted her to awareness. She rushed over, hoping that it was good news.

"Hello?" Her voice sounded hollow.

"Becca!" Her sister's voice sounded desperate. "Are you alright?" She nodded feeling a little deflated. "Answer me!" Sara almost screamed it.

"Yyy…yes." She closed her eyes, but when an image of Sean's face popped up in her mind, she opened them again on a wave of pain.

"We received a call from the Coast Guard. Sean's parents are here; they want to talk to you." When she didn't answer, Sara continued. "Becca are you up for this?" It was a whisper.

She shook her head, no, but said yes.

"Becca? Are you okay?" Lori Farrow's voice was laced with concern.

"Yyy…yes. I'm fine. I wasn't in the water with them. I was already on the boat."

"Oh, thank god! Honey don't worry. Charles and I are on the next flight down there. Just hang in until we get there. Can you do that, sweetie?"

She nodded her head as more tears escaped her eyes. Then she realized they wouldn't be able to see her answer. "Yes." It came out as a whisper.

"Good, now, here's Charles. He needs some information from you."

She nodded again. "Yes."

"Hiya there, champ." Sean's father's voice sounded like he was forcing it. "Um, we have your itinerary for the trip, but I just wanted to make sure you were still at the Lux."

She nodded and then answered, "Yes, room 404."

"Great. We should be there by eight. Becca make sure to eat something and get some rest. I plan on joining the search and hope that you'd slap on a suit and do the same. The more eyes, the better."

She straightened up. Why hadn't she gone back in the water to help? Her heart started racing. She could have found him.

"Becca?" Her sister's voice broke through the string of self-scolding. "Don't do anything stupid. You're in no shape to go anywhere right now. Just wait for the Farrows to get there."

Becca looked down at her hands and realized they were shaking so badly that she wasn't even able to hold the phone steady.

"I…I won't. I'll stay put for tonight."

"Good, I wish I could—"

"Don't. You stay there and keep my nephew or niece safe. But I could use your husband."

"He's booked on the same flight as Sean's folks are."

Becca nodded. "I'm going now." She closed her eyes and just wanted to curl up on the bed.

"Okay, get some rest. Don't worry. We'll find him. I love you, sister."

She nodded and disconnected the line. Then she walked over and since she was still shaking with cold, turned on the hot water and stripped naked. When she stepped under the spray, even the almost boiling water did little to heat her.

She must have slept. When the pounding at her door woke her, she wrapped a robe around herself and opened the door to three very worried faces.

Allen stepped in first and wrapped her in his arms. "Are you okay?" He ran his hands down her hair.

She'd thought she'd cried all she could last night, but more tears easily came. Her knees must have buckled because the next thing she knew, Allen was carrying her to a chair, where he sat down and held her close as she cried into his shoulder.

"I've ordered us some breakfast." Lori's voice broke in her thoughts.

When she glanced up through puffy, red eyes, she noticed Sean's folks were sitting across from them on the sofa. They both looked like she felt. Their eyes were red and Lori was wiping a tear away from her face with a tissue.

"I'm sorry," she said, using the robe to wipe away her tears. "I…" She stood up from Allen's lap.

"You don't have to apologize," Charles broke in. "Go ahead and get it all out." He smiled.

Lori walked over and took her in her arms and hugged her.

"I'm going to head down and see about joining the search party this morning." Allen hugged her again. "You're staying put today." He gave her a stern look. "Got it?"

She nodded, knowing she wouldn't be any help in the state she was in.

"We'll come down to the docks after we clean up." Lori patted Allen on the cheek and Becca could see a tear in her eye. "Go. Help find my boy."

He nodded, turned, and then walked out. A few minutes later, a large tray of food was delivered.

"Here we are now." Lori walked over and motioned for the woman to set the tray down between them in the sitting area. "Let's get some hot food in us and then you can shower, and we'll head downstairs." She wiped her eyes and blew her nose, then smiled over at Becca.

Becca nodded. But when she lifted the cover, nothing smelled or looked good. Actually, her stomach did a little roll and before she could blink, she was racing to the bathroom and getting sick.

"Here now, it's okay. It's just the shock," Lori said, patting her back gently as she hunched over the toilet.

She nodded her head as the woman handed her a cool washcloth.

"Maybe a nice shower first, then you can try to eat something."

Becca nodded her head again and closed her eyes as she listened to Sean's mother start her shower. "I'll leave you to it. I'll be right outside." Lori smiled down at her.

The shower helped a little. It washed away the salty

173

tears and caused her head to clear a little more. When she stepped out of the bathroom, wrapped in her robe, she quickly grabbed her bag and went to dress for the day. She pulled her hair up and brushed her teeth.

When she stepped out of the bathroom again, she felt like she might be able to eat some of the eggs and toast that had been delivered before.

"There now. How are you feeling?" Lori asked. Becca could see that the woman had been crying again but was trying to put up a front for her sake.

"I'm fine." She walked over and gave the woman a light hug. When she started to pull away, the woman just held onto her as she felt her body shake with tears.

"I'm sorry; I guess it's my turn to lose it." She looked over at her as she finally pulled away.

Becca nodded. "It's okay. It's a good thing the men aren't here to witness it." She smiled a little but felt completely hollow inside.

Lori nodded. "Eat something, and then we can head down and see what's going on."

Becca shoveled food into her mouth as quickly as she could. It helped settle the nerves that raced through her, and by the time they walked out the door, her body felt more energized.

The docks were pretty empty. It took Lori and Becca almost ten minutes before they found the small room where Ronny's mother was sitting with the search party.

Barbara rushed over to Becca and hugged her. "This is Sean's mother, Lori Farrow." She nodded to Barbara. "This is Ronny's mother, Barbara."

The women shook hands and then hugged one another. "I guess since we're in this together. Call me Lori."

"Barbara." The women smiled at one another. "Here, I was just getting an update." She nodded towards the table where three people sat. A woman and two men dressed in Coast Guard uniforms sat working on laptops.

When they walked up, the woman, who was around Becca's age, stood and nodded to them. She was shorter than Becca and had rich dark hair that hung in an intricate braid down her back.

"Miss Lander." She nodded to Becca. "We met yesterday. I'm Carmen Stanches. I'll be your eyes and ears today." The woman's accent was light and her voice was soothing enough that Becca remembered hearing it the night before.

She nodded. "This is Sean's mother, Lori Farrow."

"Mrs. Farrow." The woman nodded. "Please, sit. I'll fill you in on the morning's news."

They sat across from her as the two men continued to punch away on their computers.

"The search was called off around one last night, due to visibility. This is a standard practice and the search was picked up again just before dawn." She handed them each a bottled water. "So far, we haven't spotted anything." She continued quickly. "Which is good news. We've set up a grid." She turned her computer around. "This point"—she tapped her screen— "is where your boat was. And this"— she tapped a blue point— "this was the last place Ronny was seen and where Sean would have gone to look for him."

Becca nodded her head. "This chart shows the currents and weather." Becca watched fake waves move across the screen, and then another bubble appeared. "This is our search radius."

She closed her eyes and fear sunk in again. It was all too big. So much water to look in.

"Now, other than something else such as outside forces messing with them, the men should…"

"Outside forces?" Lori broke in.

"Sea life," Carmen said, looking down at the screen.

"I'm sorry." Becca shook her head. "I don't understand."

"Miss Lander, we're known to get an occasional shark attack. It doesn't happen often, but when…"

Becca's hearing stopped working at that point. Everything started fading to white, and she felt her entire body float away into the abyss.

## CHAPTER 18

*T*here was a loud bang, and then something terrible was stuck in front of her nose. She reached up and pushed the hand away, wanting nothing more than to sink back into the darkness.

"Here now, take deep breaths," Lori Farrow said, running her hands over Becca's face. "Easy."

"Here," a rich voice broke in. "In case she's sick."

At the thought, Becca's stomach rolled and the eggs and toast she'd shoveled into her mouth less than half an hour ago threatened to surface.

"Try some water," Ronny's mother said.

"Becca, can you sip some water?" Lori's face came into view.

She nodded her head and wished more than anything to be left alone so she could slip back into the abyss again.

When the cool water touched her tongue, she woke with full force and sat up, sputtering a little. Then she swallowed a mouthful again and felt the cold liquid spread throughout her.

She shook her head and closed her eyes. "Sharks."

"No, honey." Lori took her face in her hands and waited for Becca's eyes to meet her own. "They're okay, I just know it. Besides, Barbara's husband assured her that the water is too warm this time of year for sharks."

Becca closed her eyes and sighed. She didn't know if sharks liked warm or cold water, but just hearing the reassurance made her feel a little better.

"Do you think you can get up?"

Becca's eyes opened, and she realized she was sprawled out on the floor.

When she'd made it back to her own chair, she looked over at Carmen.

"What about my brother-in-law?" She looked off towards Barbara. "And Stan? Did they join the search?"

Carmen shook her head. "We don't allow civilians to join in the official search."

"The men rented a boat and joined it as private parties. They're searching right along with the Coast Guard," Barbara said, patting Becca's hand. "Don't worry; they're keeping us posted as well."

Becca nodded and then looked down at her watch and did a quick calculation. Twenty-two hours. Sean and Ronny had been missing for twenty-two hours now. Closing her eyes, she felt like crying.

"How long?" Her voice came out a little too soft. So, she repeated her question a little louder.

"How long until what?" Carmen asked.

"How long can a person last in the water?" She looked between the women.

"There's no set time. We've rescued people who were just slightly dehydrated after three days. The waters are warm. If they found something to use as a flotation device, there's a good chance of survival."

Becca nodded and sighed a little. "Sean's a great swimmer. Don't worry," Lori whispered. "If he found Ronny, then I'm sure the two of them are safe."

Becca nodded and then looked over to Ronny's mother. Lori was right. Sean did this kind of thing all the time. He'd told her about some of the missions he'd been on. Not the details, but the basics of what he'd been doing for the last four years.

Besides, she remembered that just before he'd returned to the water, he'd been so happy that he had finally decided that this is what he wanted to do in life.

Ronny. She closed her eyes and remembered how skinny and wiry the kid had been. If Sean hadn't gotten to the kid before…She shook her head and tried to clear those thoughts from her mind.

They sat in the small room for hours, comforting each other as they waited for any news.

Around lunchtime, they walked to the small place that served sandwiches at the entrance of the docks and grabbed some food. When they walked back into the room, Carmen updated them that she'd heard from Allen, Charles, and Stan. They were still with the Coast Guard and didn't have anything to report.

For most of the day, Becca sat in silence, feeling numb. Memories of the last few days rolled through her mind in a garbled mess. On several occasions, she caught her head rolling towards the back and her eyes closing.

"Why don't you two head back up to the room. I'll call you if we hear anything more," Barbara said softly.

Lori nodded and took Becca's hand. "Come on, honey."

Becca followed her past all the happy families splashing in the pool, past the couples walking hand in hand, and up the cold elevator. The one that she and Sean had kissed in just a short time ago.

When they walked into the room, memories flashed painfully behind her eyes.

Lori walked her over to the bed, and she sat down. Her eyes were too dry to cry anymore, so Lori sat next to her and cried for the both of them.

It was the voices that woke her. Hearing a male voice caused her to sit up quickly.

"Sean?" she screamed and looked around. Instead, she saw Allen, Charles, and Lori sitting across the room. There were trays of food and the men were shoveling it in their mouths quickly.

"I'm sorry, babe," Allen said. Setting down his fork, he walked over to her quickly. "Did we wake you?" He sat next to her and hugged her.

She shook her head, no, and held onto him.

"Anything?" she asked into his shirt.

He shook his head. "We plan on heading back down to the office and waiting until we hear something more."

She shook her head. "You need some rest." She looked between Charles and her brother-in-law. The pair of them looked exhausted.

He nodded. "Yeah, Lori was just telling us that." He

smiled a little. "I'm was just getting some food then I was going to call your sister and fill her in."

She nodded and got off the bed as Allen went back to finish his food. She walked into the bathroom and freshened up. When she looked at herself in the mirror, she was shocked. She looked like she'd lost ten pounds.

She'd gotten a nice tan during the trip, but now she was pale as a ghost. Her eyes had dark rings under them and looked hollow. Her hair was in a tangled mess and when she tried to run a brush through it, her head hurt, and she gave up. She tossed it up in a bun instead.

Sean's light jacket was on the back of the bathroom door, so she grabbed it and wrapped it around herself. She took in his scent and swore that she would never forget it. Not like Nick's.

Then her knees went weak as she realized that twice in her life she'd lost the man she loved.

By the next evening, she was exhausted. Her body wouldn't keep anything down and her mind refused to shut off unless she was on the verge of passing out. Allen had convinced Sara to demand that Becca fly home and, with the help of Sean's parents and Ronny's folks, she was strong-armed into a cab and taken to the airport with her bags in tow.

She'd refused and had even screamed and cussed at Allen at one point but, in the end, they had won.

The search would be continuing with or without her being there. Lori had gone with her as far as the security stand in the airport.

"I'll text you updates on the hour," she promised as she hugged her good-bye.

Becca had nodded, but desperately wished she could avoid getting on the plane and heading home.

When she arrived at her gate, she was half an hour early and sat down to wait. Her eyes focused straight ahead of her without really seeing anything.

Just as they called for her plane to start loading, she stood up and happened to glance at the televisions screens. Her heart skipped, then jumped so hard in her chest that her feet actually left the tile floor. Then her head was spinning as she felt the world tilt once more as sweet darkness overtook her.

# CHAPTER 19

$S$ean was fighting for more than just his life. When he pulled Ronny towards him, and he put the regulator back in his mouth, he could see his eyes roll to the back of his head. His own body was screaming for more oxygen, but years of training assured him that he could wait a few more seconds. When he saw the kid's, chest rise and fall twice, he switched over to suck in some air himself. They shared the regulator, back and forth, while they were stuck in the quicker moving currents that were dragging them farther out to sea. He tried to fight the flow, but since Ronny wasn't moving much, he just couldn't get them out of the fast-moving water.

Finally, he was able to push them to the edge of the current and felt the change in the water instantly when they were freed from the flow. As they made their way up towards the surface he continued to share his oxygen with Ronny and prayed that they hadn't strayed too far from civilization.

When they finally broke through the surface, Ronny's

body was convulsing. Sean held the kid as he upchucked water over and over. He even spit out some that had been trapped in his lungs. It felt wonderful to breathe freely again.

When the kid finally settled back down, Sean had a chance to look around for the boat. Instantly, he knew they were in trouble. Everything looked different.

They were far enough out that they had lost sight of land, so most people would have been fooled into thinking they were in the same place. But Sean knew better. The currents were different and there was the fact that there were no boats in sight.

When he'd gone back in the water for Ronny, there had been a string of diving boats that lined the coral ridge area popular for diving.

Now, as he glanced around, he couldn't make out any boats. He tossed off his heavy tank, making sure to keep any brightly colored tubes that were attached.

It was hard to hold Ronny and tie the small pieces of bright yellow plastic around their wrists, but he managed.

"You got to help me out here, buddy." He shook Ronny a little.

"I can't. I can't keep this up. I feel sick to my stomach," the boy said softly. "Where's the boat?"

Ronny looked around. His eyes were a little glazed over and red around the edges.

"Looks like we got pulled out a little way. We'll need to start kicking to get back. Think you can help?"

The kid shook his head no. "I'm spent."

"I know. That was some jolt we got back there, but we've got to…" Just then, Sean felt it, more water pushing at them. This time it was a burst of colder water from a different angle. This water was stronger and a whole lot faster as they were moved quickly down the strong current. Their bodies turned, and he held on to Ronny as they were shoved again from a different angle.

"Damn!" He growled as he locked his arms around Ronny's chest. "Hang on. Looks like we're going for another ride."

Ronny started crying and fighting against the current that was dragging them in the opposite direction. Water filled both of their mouths as they fought to stay above the surface.

"No, don't fight it," he said loudly as the water pounded their legs and chest. "We've got to move with it for a while, and then we can edge out of it." He felt the kid's legs and arms relax. "Good. When I say kick, start kicking. Don't waste all your energy; we don't know how long we'll be out here."

The kid nodded.

"Okay, kick," he yelled. They kicked their legs in sync for a while and when the water turned warmer and slowed down, they relaxed again. "Great. Good job, Ronny."

"Ron," the kid said, spitting out some water.

"Ron," Sean smiled. "What do you have on you that's bright colored?"

The kid thought about it. "There's the keychain floaty with my hotel key on it that my mom made me carry…" He broke off as he reached inside his wetsuit and pulled out a little orange life ring key chain. Sean laughed. "You know, so I wouldn't lose it. She thinks I'm such a kid."

Sean bit back a remark and tied the key ring to the kid's wrist. "Anything else?" He knew the bright yellow strip down their suits would help, but he wanted more just in case, so they wouldn't have been missed from the air.

"Nope, that's it." He sounded scared. "How deep of shit are we in?"

Sean chose not to answer right away. Instead, he moved his body behind Ron's and made sure he had a good hold of the kid. "Well, it looks like those first pushes knocked us out quite a way. Probably out past the long string of islands to the East of Nassau. The second, colder one seemed to knock us in the opposite direction. So, if my calculations are correct, we're floating right beside the long stretch of land."

"That's great. That means we can swim to shore." The kid's voice rose.

"Well, the problem is, we're pretty far out. We'll rest a while and then start kicking together." He nodded to his right. "That way."

Ron nodded. "How do you know so much?"

"It's what I do. I've spent the last four years of my life in the water working for the Special Forces."

The kid was quiet for a while. "I thought Special Forces worked on land and took out the bad guys?"

He chuckled. "Some do, and some work as divers recovering sunken secrets or infiltrating areas that boats and foot soldiers can't get to."

"Wow, really? That's cool." The kid's voice grew with excitement.

"We've got to save all the energy we can. How are you feeling?"

"Well, I was feeling a little sick at first, but I'm okay now. A little thirsty and my throat hurts."

Sean nodded, feeling the same. "We've got about three

days before dehydration sets in, but we'll be back on dry land way before then. Okay, let's start kicking together." He turned their bodies until Ron was in front of him as they floated on their backs. "Just use your legs. Ready? Go."

They kicked for roughly twenty minutes and then rested for another twenty. They did this over a dozen times and when the sun went down, the temperature of the water followed.

In between kicking, Sean floated in the water and thought of Becca and the possibility that he'd never see her again. His mind refused to accept this, and every time he started to doubt his ability, he'd start kicking again, harder and faster, so he could get back to her and hold her again.

Halfway through the night, Ron started shaking, and Sean could tell the kid was getting weaker. He took his turn kicking without his help. Sean's muscles were screaming for hydration and his stomach had stopped growling hours ago.

His head was feeling a little light, but he fought it back by focusing on an image of Becca. He continued to fight the currents during the night. He let Ron sleep, making sure to hold the kid's head above water as he took shifts kicking and resting.

When the sun rose, he made sure to point himself away from it and kick towards what he hoped was land. He glanced at his watch every so often and, out of the sheer will to live, would kick his tired legs.

Ron had been in and out of consciousness all night. The skinny kid had reached dehydration before he had, and he could feel the kid's muscles grow tighter.

Sean was so focused on seeing Becca again that when he heard the sound of a motor, it didn't register at first.

"Hey!" He started screaming and kicking his legs towards the sound, which woke Ron, who started trying to move his arms and legs. "Together," he said in the kid's ear. Ron seemed to understand, and their legs matched pace. "Raise your arms if you can," he told Ron, who tried to lift his arms above the water but was too weak.

"Over here!" he screamed when he heard the engine cut out.

It seemed to take hours, but finally, Ron's body was lifted from the water, then his own. He was too weak to help and collapsed on the deck next to Ron.

They were assaulted by a round of voices speaking in a language he didn't understand.

"English," he said weakly.

"Water," an older man said, handing him a container. He knew better than to down it quickly, and sipped it instead, then scooted over to help the kid do the same.

"He's dehydrated. He'll need a hospital." He looked around. "Can you call for help?"

The men looked at each other and then back down at him and shook their heads no. At first, Sean thought that they hadn't understood him, but then the men knelt down and picked up Ron and started to carry him below deck.

When they picked Sean up, he glanced around the boat for the first time and knew why no one was going to call for help. They'd been pulled out of the fire and straight into a furnace.

As they carried Sean downstairs and laid him next to Ron, he demanded more water and some food. The men nodded and within two minutes, water bottles and plates of broiled fish were delivered.

Sean took care of Ron, helping him sip his water and eat something first. Then he did the same for himself as the kid slept. He covered him up with blankets the men had delivered to them. Then he crawled in the bunk next to Ron and kept his eyes peeled on the kid as he slept.

One thought ran through his mind. He would make it back to Becca, even if he had to kill every man on board.

Becca felt her head spin as smelling salts were shoved in her face.

"Sean!" She sat up and screamed, then looked towards the television sets. But instead of Sean's face on them, a commercial was playing. She pushed on the man who had shoved the salts in her face. "My phone." She searched around for her bag. When she found it, she gripped for the phone and saw she'd missed five calls and too many text messages to count.

Sitting on the floor of the airport, she dialed the number and when Sean answered, she cried.

"I'm okay. We're okay," he told her over and over. Just hearing his voice made tears of joy run down her face. "We're at the hospital. Can you make it here?"

"Yes," she said and started to stand, only to be held down again by the worried man. "I'm okay," she told him. "I need to get to the hospital."

The man nodded. "An ambulance is on the way."

She shook her head and laughed. "No, I'm okay. Sean

is at the hospital." She sighed and waved the man away and then rushed over and grabbed her bags.

"Sean?" she said into the phone.

He laughed. "Still here."

"What happened?" She pushed past the security gate quickly.

"I'll explain when you get here."

"Are you okay?" she said when she finally got outside and hailed a cab.

"I'm fine. The kid's a little dehydrated still."

"Ronny? Ronny's okay?" she asked between giving the driver directions and telling him it was an emergency.

"Yup, doing fine. His folks should be here any minute."

"How?" She shook her head as the cab sped towards the hospital. "I saw you on the TV."

He chuckled. "Yeah, the news crew was here to do a piece on opening the new hospital wing. When someone spotted us walking up, I guess they recognized us from the piece they had done the day we disappeared."

"Walking up?" She shook her head not understanding. He chuckled.

"Well, me walking as I carried Ron. The guys that picked us up two days ago weren't in the mood to answer any questions from authorities. So, they dropped us off at the dock an hour ago, and we hiked from there."

"I don't understand." She closed her eyes and felt her heart race, knowing she was minutes from seeing him, holding him again.

"I'll explain later. How close are you?"

She asked the cab driver, who pointed to a large white building in front of them.

"Just pulling up outside now," she said.

"Good." She heard the phone click off and then looked up to see Sean standing in front of the glass doors with a huge smile on his lips.

He was thinner than before and looked a whole lot tanner. But he was alive.

She jumped from the car before it came to a complete stop. Then she was in his arms as he spun her around. He rained kisses over her face as she cried his name over and over.

When his mouth came down over hers, she held on to him with all the strength she had.

"I love you," they both said the second they could breathe again. Then they laughed and hugged again.

"I thought…" She shook her head.

"Here, let's go somewhere." He looked around and started pulling her inside, only to come up short when he heard someone cry his name.

He turned around and saw his parents rush towards him from a cab. Allen and Ronny's parents were close behind.

"Later," he said in her ear before he was pulled into his parents' arms.

Sean was beat. He felt like he could sleep for three days straight. That was if everyone would get out of his hotel room and leave him alone with Becca.

He looked over towards her and smiled when he noticed her eyes were on him. Her eyes turned soft and her lips curved up in a smile. She looked thinner, and he'd noticed the dark circles under her eyes at the hospital. Now he could see that she was probably as tired as he was and needed as much rest as he did.

His parents had been on the phone to everyone he knew since they'd arrived back at the room. It was a different room than Becca and he had stayed in before, but all of his stuff was there. When they had arrived, Becca had been carrying her small bag. Her larger one wasn't there and when he asked about it, she just looked over at his parents and frowned a little.

He'd talked to his sister, Dawn, his aunt, and even his cousins, assuring them all that he was well and alive.

He'd told the story of the boat of illegal fishermen who had picked Ronny and him up about eighteen hours after he'd gone back in for the kid. And of how the fishing men hadn't known what to do with the two of them, so they'd been locked in the hull of the ship for two days. When Sean had promised them that he wouldn't give the police any information about their operation, they had finally agreed to drop the two of them off at a Nassau dock.

He'd told the story so many times now, his throat was actually starting to get sore. Everyone wanted to know how he'd survived being in the water that long. Each time he was asked, he'd looked over towards Becca and smiled.

It seemed like he'd spoken to half the town of Pride since his mother had been busy calling everyone to give them the good news. She'd relayed a shorter version of the story to almost everyone he knew.

He'd even had an interesting conversation with Luke Crawford. He was shocked to hear from him that the money he'd invested in his Luke's business in high school had paid off. Big time. That was the news Luke had wanted to talk to him about before they'd left on the trip.

The surprise party that he and Amber had been planning was to celebrate that their gaming business, Modark, was holding an IPO and opening stock offerings to the public.

Which meant that his five percent share, which Luke had talked him into investing in shortly before leaving town, was now worth a chunk more. A big chunk more, if what Luke was telling him was correct. Of course, he had missed the big celebration, being lost at sea and all, but Luke assured him that he would make it up to him if he would just get his butt home.

He still couldn't wrap his mind around all of that, and when he told Becca, she just smiled and hugged him.

Later, food had been ordered and he'd eaten a whole steak and baked potato and had topped it off with a huge chunk of chocolate cake, which he'd shared with Becca.

She hadn't left his side since he'd caught hold of her at the hospital. Even when they'd talked on their phones with different people, they had held hands.

She'd said that she'd loved him, and he'd said that he'd loved her, but he desperately wished to tell her more. As soon as they were alone, he had every intention of doing just that.

"That was Barbara," his mother said, setting down the phone. "She says Ronny is up and walking about the room now, asking for food and his cell phone."

Everyone smiled. "Well, now that everyone in the world knows I'm alive...I'd like to drop off for a while." He squeezed Becca's hand and smiled over at her.

"Oh, you must be exhausted," his mother piped in.

"Here we've been taking up all your time." She walked over and hugged him and gave him another kiss on his cheek. A tear slid down her face so he gently wiped it with the back of his hand.

"I'm okay. Go, get some rest yourself." He smiled at her.

She nodded. "Dinner, tonight. Downstairs around six."

He looked over at Becca, who nodded.

"Make it seven." He smiled when his mother nodded and brushed his hair away from his eyes.

"It's time for a trim." She tugged his hair lightly.

He ran his hands through his hair and smiled. "I kind of like it longer."

"So do I," Becca said beside him.

His father gave him a bear hug and patted his back. "You sure did scare the heck out of us, son." He pulled back quickly and glared at him. "Don't do it again."

He laughed and nodded. "Yes, sir."

He shook Allen's hand at the door and when he shut it, made sure to flip the privacy lock.

"So…" He turned back to the room and smiled when he saw Becca standing a few feet away, smiling at him. "Where were we?"

"I love you," she said softly. "And you love me." Her smile grew.

"Yes, I do." He took a step towards her and watched her eyes moisten. "But there's more. While I was floating in the water, completely out of control of my own destiny, I promised myself one thing."

Her eyebrows shot up in question. She was gripping her hands in front of her tightly. He took another step towards her.

"I promised myself that if I got out of it alive, that I would take what I wanted without question. I would do all the things I've always wanted and never look back."

She smiled a little more and nodded. "Sounds like a good plan."

He stopped a foot away from her and then slowly knelt before her as he took her hands in his.

"Becca Beatrice Lander"—she cringed at her middle name— "help me fulfill my deepest desires. Become my wife so we can buy a house in Pride, and I can help you through school to get your degree and become a history teacher. I can teach diving school and we can raise our three kids, two dogs, chickens, and whatever else. So we can live happily ever after."

Tears were streaming down her cheeks. She used her free hand to wipe them away as she nodded her head.

"Yes, of course, I'll marry you, Sean Thomas Farrow." She smiled at him. "On one condition." His heart dropped a little.

"Anything." He felt his mouth go dry, waiting.

"We get married before we leave here." She took his face in her hands and leaned down to kiss him. "I've waited a lifetime for you to return to me. I don't want to wait another moment."

He smiled and slowly stood up, pulling her into his arms. "Anything," he whispered before he took her lips with his.

# EPILOGUE

*J*ust before the sunset two nights later, Becca walked out of the hotel lobby. The simple cream dress she wore flowed around her legs as she walked.

She smiled at her brother-in-law as he held his arm out for her to hold onto. As they walked past friends and family, her eyes focused on Sean, who stood by a large archway that was covered in flowers. He was very tan and had recently gotten a haircut. He looked so dashing in his cream cotton suit as he waited for her.

Ronny stood beside him with a huge smile on his face and looked very handsome in his matching cream-colored jacket and pants.

When they stopped in front of the preacher, Sean took her hand in his and tugged until she almost fell into his arms. Then he placed a kiss solidly on her lips. Everyone laughed and cheered. She pulled back from him with a huge smile on her lips.

"Sorry, I just had to get that out of the way." Sean smiled and then nodded to the preacher to begin.

As they stood there with the sun sinking lower over the clear waters, tourists stopped to watch the small wedding party. Many people continued to splash in the waters nearby and kids played in the warm sand.

When the vows were finished, and the rings exchanged, Sean leaned in and kissed Becca once more. This time she held onto him just a little longer, knowing it would last forever.

PREVIEW – LOVING LAUREN

PROLOGUE

Hot wind whirled around Lauren's skirt, causing it to fly up. She laughed as she twirled around. Stopping for a second to catch her breath, she looked over at her sisters, Alex and Haley. Alex's bright blonde head was pointed downward as she sat in the dirt, happily making a mud pile. Haley's dark curly hair lay in the grass as she watched the clouds rush by.

Lauren looked up at the sky and noticed that the clouds were going by very fast. Frowning a little, she decided that dancing some more while keeping her eyes glued to the sky might be fun. She twirled while watching everything rush by her, almost causing her to tumble over and fall.

Dancing in the fields was one of her greatest joys. Even though she had to babysit her younger sisters today, she didn't mind. For the most part, her sisters could enter-tain themselves. Lauren still had to carry Haley sometimes when her short legs got tired. She supposed that being four was tiring, though she couldn't remember ever being four. She thought she must have slept through her life until she turned five when her first memories happened. Haley was always asleep, or lying down, like now. But Lauren was eight and she had enough energy to shake the roof off the barn, or so her Daddy always said.

The breeze moved the tall grass around them, making the field look as if it were dancing with her. She stopped to bow to her make-believe dance partner, a move she'd seen late one night when she had sneaked to the edge of the stairs. Her parents had been watching an old black-and-white movie and she could make out the screen if she tilted her head just right. The woman in the long white dress had bowed slowly while smiling at a tall gentleman in a black suit and tie. They'd looked so wonderful. From that moment on, Lauren had wanted to dance. Every chance she had, she'd moved around like she'd watched the couple do, wishing her dress was longer so it would flow like the ladies had.

Taking a break, she looked off towards the house. The large three-story stone place sat like a beacon in the yellow fields. Its bright white pillars gleamed in the sunlight, at least when the clouds weren't shadowing the land. It was the only place she'd ever known as home. Her dad's dad had built the place a long, long time ago. Probably a zillion years ago. The outside looked new, and her dad did every-thing he could to keep the inside looking new, too. But Lauren knew some of the floorboards creaked when you walked on them. And the water only stayed hot long enough for her and her sisters to share a bath at night. But worst of all, she had blue carpet in her bedroom. Lauren hated blue. She'd begged her dad for new carpet, yellow preferably. Her dad told her it was blue because it used to be his room, and that it would have to stay blue until they could afford new carpet. Her room was perfect, except for the blue carpet. It was like a big wart on her room. Not that she'd ever gotten warts. Jenny Steven's had a wart once on her finger and she had to wear a My Little Pony Band-Aid over it. But during recess, Jenny had pulled the Band-Aid off and shown Lauren her wart. It was gross, all wet and puffy. So, Lauren thought of her blue carpet as a wart on the face of her bedroom.

Looking at the house, she knew her mama was back in the kitchen making a feast for the church potluck tomorrow. Everyone was going to be there, even Dale Bennett. She didn't like Dale; he always pulled her hair and pushed her into the dirt, even when she was wearing her new church dress.

She knew that her mama was the best cook in the county. Or so her daddy always said.

Hearing a loud noise, she looked off towards the dark clouds that were forming over the hills. Her daddy was somewhere up in the hills, gathering the cows. She didn't know why they had to move the cows around all the time. It was still a mystery to her why they couldn't just stay here in the fields. There was plenty of tall grass to eat right here, close to the house. Another loud sound came from the hills. At first, Lauren thought it was a gunshot. She'd heard a lot of those growing up on the huge ranch, but then she turned her head a little and heard her mother screaming for them.

"Girls! Run, come quick!" Her mother stood in the front door, her apron flowing in the wind as her hands motioned for them to come to her.

"Come on. Mama wants us to run," Lauren told her sisters.

Alex stood and dusted off her hands and started skipping towards the house. Haley, on the other hand, didn't move.

"Come on, Haley, Mama wants us to run home." Another loud noise came from behind her and when she looked, the sky had turned black. Fear shot through her like a bolt of lightning. Without saying a word, Lauren grabbed up her baby sister and started running. Since her legs were longer than Alexis,' she made it to her skipping sister and screamed for her to run faster. Halfway to the house, Lauren had to set Haley down. Her little sister had gained a few pounds and was too heavy for her to carry the entire way. Their mother wasn't in the doorway when they got there; instead, she was standing in the hallway.

"Quick, we have to get to the shelter." Her mother picked up Haley and started running towards the back door.

"Mama, Bear!" Haley screamed. "I want Bear!"

Their old deaf dog was lying by the fireplace, where he always stayed, taking a nap.

"Fine." Their mother set Haley down next to her and looked Lauren in the eyes. At this time, Lauren could hear the wind rushing through the house. The sound was so loud that Haley covered her ears and started to cry. "Lauren, I want you to make sure you get your sisters into the shelter like I taught you. Can you do that?"

Lauren remembered the drills Mama and Papa had put her through. Nodding her head, she grabbed her sisters' hands. "Yes, Mama."

"Good. Now run," her mother yelled over the noise, then she took off down the hallway to grab the dog as Lauren turned and started running, dragging her sisters behind her. When they got to the kitchen, Alex stopped. She pulled her hand out of Lauren's and started grabbing cookies that their mother had been baking.

"No, Alex, we have to go now." Lauren dropped Haley's hand and grabbed Alex by the shoulders, causing her to drop all the cookies.

"No, I'm gonna tell Mama." Alex started crying. Here in the back of the house, the noise was even louder. She could see grass and leaves fly by the windows when she looked out.

"We have to get to the shelter, or Mama is going tell Daddy." That stopped her sister from picking up the dropped cookies. Lauren grabbed her hand and turned back to get Haley, but Haley was gone. Just then their mother came into the kitchen carrying the old dog.

"Where's Haley?" she screamed, as she held the old dog in her arms.

"I don't know. She was just here. Then Alex—"

"Here, we don't have time for stories now. Take Bear and Alex and get to the shelter. Run girls, run!" Her mother pushed Bear into her arms. The dog looked small in her mother's arms, but in hers, he was heavy. She had to shift his fat body to make sure she didn't drop him. Alex ran to the back door and opened it. Hearing her mother's urgent tone, she must have understood that something bad was happening.

The girls rushed across the backyard through the high wind and the heavy rain that was falling. When they reached the storm shelter, Lauren had to set Bear down to open the big door. Alex grabbed Bear's collar, making sure he didn't run away as Lauren pushed the door open. Then Alex pulled Bear down the stairs as Lauren looked back towards the house. She could see a light go on in her sister's bedroom, and then her mother's shadow crossed the window. Her mother bent down, and when she stood back up, Lauren could see that Haley was in her arms. She felt relieved until she looked up.

"Run, Mama!" Lauren screamed. The dark clouds circled above the house, and Lauren's little body froze to the spot outside the shelter. It seemed like hours later when her mother finally appeared at the back door holding Haley. Her sister's head was buried in her mother's apron.

"Get inside!" her mother screamed halfway across the backyard.

Lauren's feet became unglued and she rushed to the bottom of the stairs. Turning, she waited for her mother to reach the shelter door. She watched as her mother's dress flew sideways in the high winds. Haley was holding onto her apron tightly.

Then everything slowed down in Lauren's mind. Her mother, a few steps from the doorway, looked up quickly, then turned her head and looked right at her. Lifting Haley high, she threw her into the open doorway. Haley fell down the stairs, and her little body hit Lauren's with enough force that it knocked them down. Haley's body shook as she cried, still clutching a piece of their mother's apron, which had been ripped from her shoulders. Lauren quickly got up and stood on the floor of the shelter, looking up into the doorway. She watched in terror as the ferocious winds ripped her mother from the doorway and swept her into the darkness.

# LOVING LAUREN

## CHAPTER 1

*T*en years later...

Lauren looked down at the grave as a tear slipped down her nose. It was a week before her nineteenth birthday, and she watched as her father's closest friends lowered his casket into the ground. She heard her sisters crying beside her and blindly reached over and took both of their hands. It had been two days since she'd found her father lying on his bedroom floor. She'd done everything she'd known to try and save him, but she'd been too late. She'd do anything to go back and somehow get to the house earlier that sunny day.

Closing her eyes, she could remember her father's face, his kindness, the way he moved and smelled, and the way he talked. Everything about the man had told his daughter's that he loved them, that he'd do anything for them. They'd lost their mother ten years ago; their father had picked up the pieces and raised three girls on his own. They had all missed their mother, but thanks to their father, they had grown up knowing that they were loved. They had never gone to bed hungry, dirty, or without a bedtime story.

If the food had been a little burned or a little odd tasting, the girls never complained. Even when Alex's costume for the school play had turned out looking more like a green leaf than a tree, she hadn't complained. When Lauren had finally hit the age to legally drive, she'd taken it upon herself to drive her sisters to and from school and any other after school functions they'd been involved in, even if it meant forgoing her own social life.

The guilt had always played in the back of her mind. *If I had just watched Haley better. If I had just kept holding her hand, Mama would be here today.*

The school had offered the girls counseling, but Lauren had just sat through it and had told the older woman who had been assigned to counsel her what she'd wanted to hear. Not once did she hint that it was her fault that their mother was gone. Not once did she confide in anyone that she was to blame.

When her father was in the ground, she closed her eyes and lifted her face to the sky. The spring Texas air felt wonderful. She knew that in a little over a month, the breeze would be hot enough to steam the tears that were falling down her face. The cool wind would stop and be replaced by stillness and heat. But for now, she enjoyed the smell of the grass growing, the flowers blooming, and the sight of the cherry trees that were planted around the small cemetery. Her father had always loved the spring. He'd been looking forward to helping her plant a new flower garden near the back of the house.

Now, who was she going to plant flowers with? She opened her eyes and looked at Alexis. Her blonde hair was tied up in a simple bun at the base of her neck. Her black skirt and gray shirt were in complete contrast to her sister's normal attire. Even though Alex had just turned sixteen, her wild side had been on the loose for the last two years. So much so that it had started eating up a lot of Lauren's and their father's time.

*"Your sister is going to be the death of me. Mark my words, Lauren. Someday you're going to walk in and she'll be standing over my cold body, complaining about the fact that she can't have a pair of hundred-dollar jeans."*

In fact, Alex hadn't been home that day. She'd stayed the night at a friend's house that entire weekend.

Lauren looked over at Haley. She was too young to remember their mother. And even though they'd never talked about it, she knew her sister was a little jealous of the fact that Lauren and Alex could both remembered her.

As the minister, a longtime family friend was saying his closing, Lauren looked down at her father's final resting place. What was she going to do now? How were they going to live without him?

Her shoulders sank a little as she walked forward and tossed a white rose into the hole, onto her father's casket. When she turned and stepped away, she looked off to the distance. West of here was Saddleback Ranch, their home for as long as she could remember. It had been handed down for three generations now.

Straightening her shoulders and looking off to the distance, she knew in her heart that she'd do anything-anything-to keep it. To keep her and her sisters together. On their land. Like her father and mother would have wanted her to do.

After shaking the hands of and hugging almost

everyone in the small three-thousand-person strong community, she stood outside her truck talking briefly with Grant Holton Sr., her father's lawyer and one of his best friends. Mr. Holton was tall and very broad chested. She'd heard once that he and her father had played football together.

She looked over as Dr. Graham and his son, Chase, walked up to them. Dr. Graham had been the ranch's veterinarian. Every animal on her land was healthy thanks to the older man who walked forward and shook her hand with a firm grip. Chase had been a year ahead of her in school. They'd grown up together and had even gone to a couple dances together in high school and had shared a few stolen kisses behind the bleachers. But then he'd graduated and she'd seen less and less of him.

Chase was tall like his father. It looked like he'd tried to grease back his bushy mass of black hair for the ceremony. She'd always loved pushing her hands into his thick hair. His dark brown eyes stared at her with sincere concern and grief, much like his father's did now.

"Lauren." Dr. Graham shook her hand, then Mr. Holton's.

Mr. Holton nodded and then turned towards her. "I know this isn't the time to think about your future or the ranch's future, but maybe we can meet tomorrow. Just the three of us. There are a few details I need to go over with you."

At that moment, the realization hit her—she was the head of the house. She was now in charge of a thousand-acre ranch. In charge of her sisters. In charge of the cattle, the horses, everything. She must have paled a little because Chase stepped forward and took her elbow. "Are you okay?" he whispered.

She wanted to shove his arm away and scream. "No! I'm not okay, you idiot. Everything is ruined! I have no family left." But instead, she nodded and swayed a little, causing him to move his other arm around her waist. "Dad," Chase said, looking towards his father.

"Quite right, we apologize." The older man cleared his throat, looking towards his friend.

"No," Lauren blinked. If she wanted to keep the three of them on her family's land, she would just have to step up a little more. Remember, she told herself, keep your sisters together and do whatever it takes to stay on your family's land. "If you want, I'm heading back to the house now. We can meet in say"—she looked at her watch as Chase dropped his arm— "an hour?"

Dr. Graham and Mr. Holton nodded their heads in unison. She could see the questions in their eyes. Lauren turned when she spotted her sisters walking towards her. She walked stiffly around to the driver's side of her truck, her shoulders square. As they drove away in silence, she looked back and saw the three men standing there. A shiver rolled down her back and she knew at that moment that everything was going to change.

The drive to the ranch wasn't a long one. It sat almost ten miles outside of town, but the roads were always empty, and the highway stretched in a straight line. When they passed the old iron gate with Saddleback Ranch overhead, she felt a little peace settle in her bones. There, in the distance, stood the three-story house she'd always known and loved. It had taken some bangs in its time. The tornado that had claimed their mother had torn the roof right off the massive place. The old red barn had been flattened back then as well. They'd lost a dozen horses and two of the farmhand houses. Thank goodness her father and the men had been in the hills that day, or they might have been caught up in the storm as well. But the barn and farmhands' houses had been rebuilt. The house had gotten a shiny new roof, along with a new paint job and some new windows panes to replace the ones that had blown out. After her father replaced the storm cellar's door, no one talked about that day anymore.

Lauren stopped the truck in front of the barn, and Haley jumped out and ran through the massive doors. Alex turned and looked at Lauren.

"Don't worry. I'll go talk to her." Lauren patted her sister's thigh and got out of the truck. Dingo, the family dog, an Australian shepherd mix, rushed up to Lauren and jumped on her dress. "No, down." She pushed the dog off, but she followed her into the dark barn.

Outside, the sun had warmed her, but here in the darkness of the barn, the coolness seeped into her bones. She rubbed her arms with her hands as she walked forward to climb the old stairs that led to the second floor, where she knew her sister would be.

The loft was huge, taking up three-quarters of the barn, but Lauren knew Haley's hiding places and walked right to her sister. Haley was stretched out on the soft hay, her best Sunday dress fanned out around her. She was face down and crying like there was no tomorrow. Lauren walked over and sat next to her. She pulled her into her arms and cried with her.

Less than an hour later, Lauren had changed into her

work clothes and stood at the door to greet Mr. Holton, Dr. Graham, and, to her surprise, Chase. The four of them walked into her father's large office and she shut the glass doors behind her. Taking a large breath, she turned to face the room.

"Please, have a seat." She motioned for the three men to sit as she walked around her father's massive desk and sat in his soft leather chair. She'd done it a hundred times, but this time it felt different.

"Your father was a great man," Mr. Holton started. "He was our best friend." He looked at Dr. Graham, and the other man nodded his head in agreement. "We could postpone this meeting for—"

"No, please." Lauren straightened her shoulders.

"Very well." Mr. Holton pulled out a file from his briefcase. "As you know, I am your father's lawyer. John, here"—he nodded to Dr. Graham— "well, he has a stake in what we need to discuss. That's why I invited him along."

"Continue," Lauren said when she thought Mr. Holton had lost his nerve. She knew it was bad news; she could see it clearly on both man's faces.

"Well, after that day"—Mr. Holton cleared his throat and shifted in his seat— "after we lost your mother, Richard took out some loans."

"Mr. Holton how much did my father owe the bank?" She wanted the bottom line. Holding her breath, she waited.

"Well, that's the tricky part. You see, Richard didn't trust in banks all that much." The two older men looked between themselves. "Maybe this will explain it better." He set the file on the desk in front of her.

She opened the file with shaky fingers. There, in her father's handwriting, was her future.

I, Richard West, being of sound body and mind, do solemnly promise to pay back the total sum of $100,000.00 to Johnathan Graham Sr. and Grant Holton II. If anything should happen to me, the proceeds of my ranch, Saddleback Ranch, would go to both men in equal amounts until paid back in full. They would have a say in the running of the ranch until said amount was paid in full.

It had been dated and signed by her father, John Graham, and Grant Holton Sr. over ten years ago.

"I understand your concerns." She looked up from the paper. "As head of the house now, I will fulfill my father's obligations."

"Well, that's all well and good." Dr. Graham smiled. "But, well, we had an understanding between the three of us. If anything happened to him and we saw that you three or the ranch was in any jeopardy, we'd step in and run this place until we saw fit."

Lauren listened as the men told her the scheme the three of them—her father, Mr. Holton and Dr. Graham—had come up with ten years ago in case anything like this should happen. How they'd take over the running of the land, the handling of the finances, even deciding how to deal with her and her sisters. She was being pushed out before she'd even had the chance to try and run things her way. She'd practically raised her sisters, and now these two men wanted to take control of everything, even her. Her heart sank upon hearing this news. She asked for some time to think about it and the men apologized and quickly excused themselves.

After the older men had driven away, Chase stayed

behind and offered her another option. The next day Lauren stood in front of the courthouse in Tyler, wearing her Sunday best. She knew her life would never be the same again after that day.

Seven years later…

Chase stood in the middle of the street and took a deep breath. He was finally home. It wasn't that he'd been avoiding the place, or that he hadn't had the will to return, but life had led him down a twisted path. He was happy that he'd finally ended up back here, at least for now. A car horn honked at him, and he waved and moved from the center of the road. Walking up the stone steps to his father's building, he realized that the old green place had never looked better. He knew the money he'd been sending home over the last nine years had helped with fixing up the clinic.

When he opened the front door, the bell above the door chimed and he smiled.

"Morning, how can I—" Cheryl, his father's receptionist, stood slowly. "Son of a…"

"Now, Cheryl, you know you're not supposed to say that around here." He walked forward and received her welcome hug. The woman almost engulfed him, but he smiled and took the beating as she patted his back hard. Her arms were like vices, but her front was soft and she smelled just like he remembered, like chocolate and wet puppies. The odd mix of aromas had always warmed his spirits.

"What are you doing back in town?" she asked. She

gasped. "Does your father know?" She looked towards the back room.

He shook his head. "I wanted to surprise him." He smiled.

Her smile slipped a little. "Well, you sure will." Then she bit her bottom lip and he knew something was up.

"Spill." He took her shoulders before she could turn away.

"What?" She tried to look innocent.

"Cheryl, how long have I known you?"

She smiled. "Going on twenty-eight years next June." He smiled. Cheryl always did remember his birthday.

"And in all that time, I've come to know that when you bite your bottom lip, you have something you're trying to hide. So..."—he motioned with his hand— "spill."

She crossed her arms over her chest. "Fine. It's just your father's health. I know he hasn't mentioned it over the phone to you."

"What about it?" Chase began to get worried and felt like rushing to the back room to check up on his dad. Cheryl had never mentioned anything personal about his father's health in their conversations. Neither had his father.

"Well, he injured his leg a while back." She twisted her shirtfront.

"And?" He waited.

"And, well, he's walking with a cane now," she blurted out, just as his father walked through the back door.

"Thank you, Cheryl. That will be enough out of you." His father smiled. Sure enough, his father was leaning on a black cane. "Well, boy?" He held out his arm. "Don't make me hobble over to you for that hug."

Chase rushed across the room and gave his old man a bear hug like he always had, noticing that his father was not only skinnier but felt frailer. He had a million questions he wanted to ask but knew his father wouldn't answer until he was good and ready.

"Come on back here, boy. Tell me what you've been up to." His father started walking towards the back and Chase watched him hobble. Then his father turned. "Are you back to stay?"

"Yes," Chase said absentmindedly. He hadn't meant to stay, had he?

"Good." His father turned into his office and took a seat, setting the cane down beside him. Chase sat in the chair across from him, waiting.

"Well, I suppose I should tell you, you couldn't have come home at a better time. I'm retiring."

"What?" Chase sat up. His father raised his hands, holding off the million questions he had.

"Yes, at the end of the year. I've been kicked one too many times." His father smiled. "This old body doesn't want to work like it used to. I was going to give you a call later this month."

"Dad?" He looked at him.

"I know, I know. I told you I'd never retire, but..." he looked down at his leg. "The doctors are telling me I have to be off this damned leg for six hours a day. Six! You and I both know that in this line of work you'd be lucky to sit for five minutes a day."

Chase smiled. "I guess it's a good thing I'm home, then."

His father smiled and nodded his head. "What do you say we go grab some lunch? I'm buying."

Fairplay, Texas, had one place to sit and eat. Mama's Diner, a huge brown barn that had been turned into a restaurant, had been the best place to eat in two counties since as far back as Chase could remember. Even now the place looked new and smelled like greasy burgers.

His father took his usual booth. It almost made Chase laugh, knowing the man never sat in a different spot. Even if someone was in it, he'd stand and wait until the table was cleared. There were new menus and he took his time looking over the list of new items.

"How are you today, beautiful?" his father asked the waitress when she stopped by.

Chase looked up and stared into the most beautiful green eyes he'd ever seen. Her hair was longer than before, and her dark curls hung just below the most perfect breasts he'd ever had the pleasure of being up against. She was tall and limber and he could remember the softness of every curve he'd been allowed to feel. She looked down at him like he was in her way and he started coughing. He couldn't explain how it happened, but he was choking on air. Nothing was getting through to his lungs or to his brain. Finally, she smacked his back hard, and he took a deep breath. He stood and grabbed Lauren's arm and demanded in a low voice, "What the hell are you doing working here?"

This is a work of fiction. Names, characters, places, and incidents either are the product of the author's imagination or are used fictitiously, and any resemblance to actual persons, living or dead, business establishments, events or locales is entirely coincidental.

RETURN TO ME

DIGITAL ISBN: 978-1-942896-01-2

PRINT ISBN: 978-1511454025

Copyright © 2015 Jill Sanders

All rights reserved.

Copyeditor: InkDeepEditing.com

ALSO BY JILL SANDERS

**The Pride Series**

Finding Pride

Discovering Pride

Returning Pride

Lasting Pride

Serving Pride

Red Hot Christmas

My Sweet Valentine

Return To Me

Rescue Me

**The Secret Series**

Secret Seduction

Secret Pleasure

Secret Guardian

Secret Passions

Secret Identity

Secret Sauce

**The West Series**

Loving Lauren

Taming Alex

Holding Haley

Missy's Moment

Breaking Travis

Roping Ryan

Wild Bride

Corey's Catch

Tessa's Turn

## The Grayton Series

Last Resort

Someday Beach

Rip Current

In Too Deep

Swept Away

High Tide

## Lucky Series

Unlucky In Love

Sweet Resolve

Best of Luck

A Little Luck

## Silver Cove Series

Silver Lining

French Kiss

Happy Accident

Hidden Charm

A Silver Cove Christmas

**Entangled Series – Paranormal Romance**

The Awakening

The Beckoning

The Ascension

**Haven, Montana Series**

Closer to You

Never Let Go

Holding On

**Pride Oregon Series**

A Dash of Love

My Kind of Love

Season of Love

Tis the Season

Dare to Love

Where I Belong

**Wildflowers Series**

Summer Nights

Summer Heat

**Stand Alone Books**

Twisted Rock

For a complete list of books:

http://JillSanders.com

# ABOUT THE AUTHOR

*Jill Sanders is a New York Times, USA Today, and international bestselling author of Sweet Contemporary Romance, Romantic Suspense, Western Romance, and Paranormal Romance novels. With over 55 books in eleven series, translations into several different languages, and audiobooks there's plenty to choose from. Look for Jill's bestselling stories wherever romance books are sold or visit her at jillsanders.com*

*Jill comes from a large family with six siblings, including an identical twin. She was raised in the Pacific Northwest and later relocated to Colorado for college and a successful IT career before discovering her talent for writing sweet and sexy page-turners. After Colorado, she decided to move south, living in Texas and now making her home along the Emerald Coast of Florida. You will find that the settings of several of her series are inspired by her time spent living in these areas. She has two sons and off-set the testosterone in her house by adopting three furry little ladies that provide her company while she's locked in her writing cave. She enjoys heading to the beach, hiking, swimming, wine-tasting, and pickleball with her husband, and of course writing. If you have read any of her books, you may also notice that there is a love of food, especially sweets! She has been blamed for a few added pounds by her assistant, editor, and fans… donuts or pie anyone?*

facebook.com/JillSandersBooks

twitter.com/JillMSanders

bookbub.com/authors/jill-sanders

Made in the USA
Monee, IL
18 April 2021

66130170R00128